Robert Harbinson was born in Belfast in 1928 and educated in Enniskillen. Before becoming a professional writer, he had a variety of jobs including Belfast shipyard worker and cabin boy on a dredger. He was later to study at Barry Religious College in Wales and went to Canada as a missionary. Later in Canada, he worked as a trapper and as a teacher. He is perhaps best known for his autobiographical quartet: *No Surrender* (1960), *Song of Erne* (1960), *Up Spake the Cabin Boy* (1961) and *The Protégé* (1963). He has published two collections of short stories: *Tattoo Lily and Other Ulster Stories* (1961) and *The Far World and Other Stories* (1962). Under the name 'Robert Bryans' he has written many travel books and further autobiographical works. He currently lives in England.

By the same author

SELECTED STORIES

SELECTED STORIES

ROBERT HARBINSON

edited by John Keyes

LAGAN PRESS
BELFAST
2005

Published by
Lagan Press
1A Bryson Street
Belfast BT5 4ES
e-mail: lagan-press@e-books.org.uk
web: lagan-press.org.uk

ISBN: 1 873687 06 0
(First edition 1996, reprinted with minor corrections 2005)
Authors: Harbinson, Robert
Title: Selected Stories
(edited by John Keyes)
2005

Set in Goudy
Printed by Biddles Printers, Norwich

To Jeanie Keys—
whose mother, Mary Neill, features in my later work
and whose memory is a bright image of my childhood
in Donegall Avenue

Contents

Preface

A rush of nostalgia overwhelmed me then, and remorse for treating Gertie badly. What hours we had spent on that little beach, so far away now. The sea air sharpened my appetite and I opened her hamper. How beautifully everything was packed. I thought of her in the farm kitchen that morning, carefully preparing the basket, laying everything in place. The bread alone brought memories. I knew that never another griddle would bake such delicious golden meal farls as did Gertie's—just as mown hay on the sundown airs would never rise so sensuous as on that final walk with her to the spring well. Now she would be on her way back to the farm, for the milking. Later, she would be giving the cats their supper in the sweet smelling barn. By the time I got the train in Scotland she would take a last look in the hayshed, then the back door would be bolted for the night.

Satan was at work, I knew, in conjuring up these pictures in my mind. But, nevertheless, I did not take out my Bible to look up the texts Gertie had written on the hardboiled eggs. Instead I cracked the shells, and threw them overboard. I watched them float down to the churning water. For a moment they rode the surface. Then the foam took them under.

The words are from the end of Robert Harbinson's third volume of autobiography, *Up Spake the Cabin Boy*. They were his farewell to home, for, though Ireland is at the centre of all his best work, apart from periodic visits over the years, he has always lived somewhere else.

Yet there is a sense in which he has never left and even in his most eccentric wanderings, even in the bizarre circumstances in which he later found himself, there is a tone which is at once Irish and international.

He was born Robin Bryans in east Belfast, just off the Newtownards Road, in 1928. When he was five months old the family moved up the social ladder, if only a little, and made the trek across Belfast to Donegall Avenue, at that time on the very boundary of the city. Now, instead of shipyard workers streaming along Dee Street to the Queen's Island, the predominant influence on young Robin Bryans was the railway which ran along the backs of the small parlour house terrace, shaking the walls, rattling the dishes, leaving soot everywhere.

But if the railway at the back, shaking the foundations of the houses, suggested the Dickensian squalor of *Dombey and Son*, the vista at the front facing the south-west was more pleasing, less constricted.

No other street in the city was so clearly emblematic of the contradictions of Belfast itself. Respectable, working-class, Protestant, it had the virtues as well as the faults of similar communities throughout Belfast. Small, costly acts of impoverished charity; a rough kindness and, of course, censoriousness and the firm conviction of being right and decent in a chaotic world. Donegall Avenue was, above all, respectable. The avenue was broad and tree-lined; the houses, for the most part, the traditional two-up and two-down, with the lavatory and coal house discreetly out of sight at the end of the backyard. Newer houses had an attic and were much sought after by the larger working-class families with ten or more children to be clothed and slept.

The railway track provided perquisites as well as noise and dirt. Coal was shed along the lines by the constant trains. Thrifty women were up and along the tracks in the early dark before the dawn, gathering what fuel they could to warm their families. Respectable women, wrapped in black shawls—led by my grandmother, Mary Neill—walked the lines, their eyes fixed on the ground, big bags open to receive the unburnt coal. Backache was endemic; chest complaints widespread. Wash days were a nightmare, for the dazzling washing, first boiled, then scrubbed on washboards by hand, strenuously rolled through heavy mangles and hung high in the small yards, could be drenched with soot from the belching trains and many hours of back-breaking work would go for nothing.

The tracks provided adventure as well as an anvil on which budding young capitalists might lay the foundations of future fortune or, at least, enable the purchase of present necessities.

A halfpenny, commonly known as a 'wing', placed on the railtrack, and passed over by a train, would miraculously expand to the dimensions of a penny (a 'make') and could, when inserted into one of the new dispensing machines, often yield up a delicious bar of chocolate. The Dublin train was considered the most suitable to effect this translation. The bushes growing thickly along the rail embankment provided excellent cover for boys avoiding hot pursuit by angry parents or vexatious sorties by the police whose understanding of high spirits was disappointingly low.

And there were even greater challenges to be met. The bravest of the boys found here precisely the most daring rituals through which they might establish their manhood to their guardians and their leadership among their peers. The procedure was simplicity itself. Methodology was undemanding intellectually, though stimulating to the nerves.

Decisiveness and resolution were all that was required. The boy, accompanied by a noisy and nervous escort, would lie on his back between the iron rails, his escort wisely remaining hidden in the shrubs. A faint hum, a tiny vibration, a building excitement warned of the approaching train. This was the moment that called for the steeliest nerves, the firmest self-control. It was essential that the boy concerned should lie without movement as the train passed over him. An untoward reaction, a reflexive jerk, or even sheer and unexpected terror would result in death and possible decapitation. But there could be no doubt in anyone's mind as the train sped off that the boy was now a man.

My father's mother, deaf and dumb from birth, gave utterance to the only recorded sound she ever made when, crossing a wooden bridge, her arms full of potatoes and flour, she saw my father disappear, head, torso and finally feet under a shrieking train. Potatoes ricocheted along the track and flour ascended in a mystic cloud as she, for the only time in her life, screamed at the top of a non-existent voice. There is no record of the subsequent scene between my father and his mother, but family history holds that it was disagreeable.

Of all the wild boys of Donegall Avenue, it was commonly agreed among the neighbours that Robin Bryans was the wildest. Heads were shaken, more in sorrow than in anger, as Bryans' escapades became more and more colourful. And if young Robin, in his peregrinations through the Donegall Road and Sandy Row areas of the town, had not discovered the excitement of religion his fate might have been very different. But the Protestant areas were rich in 'wee free' halls, where evangelic preachers of the Word exhorted young and old to come to Jesus. The future they depicted for those who failed to take up their offer of future bliss in exchange for present slavery was gloomy.

The hellfire preachers were, from the point of view of entertainment, excellent value. Their pictures of the fires of hell, not to mention constant and enjoyably virtuous references to the gnashing of teeth, were graphic, and could scarcely fail to inspire feelings of pity and terror. Of course, such sensations could properly be enjoyed only if one had been 'saved' and 'born again', thus ensuring that one could reflect comfortably upon the sum of human wickedness, exemplified by boys like Robin Bryans or the woman at the bottom of the Avenue who, it was well known, was not only no better than she should be, but, in addition, smoked twenty Craven A cigarettes every single week. From the safe shores of a happy land surrounded by saints in glory giving vent to the occasional 'hallelujah', the parlous state of Man, not to mention the peculiar caprices of the Almighty, might be enjoyed.

The mission halls were the theatres of the impoverished Protestant classes. They provided drama, entertainment, not unenjoyable terror, and a nice cup of tea and a bun after the rigours of repentance, well known to sharpen the appetite. There was warmth, community, the rousing, often bloodthirsty hymns and, above all, a pleasing sense of being set apart, of being 'saved'.

They appealed greatly to young Robin, who was comfortably 'saved' on a number of occasions and enjoyed frequent states of grace which he found gratifying though, on the whole, a little tedious.

But it was on the other side of Donegall Avenue that Robin Bryans found the real magic of the world. Behind the row of houses facing his own, lay the Bog Meadows:

> But the rows of houses did not go on for ever. Beyond them lay the Bog Meadows' marshy steppes where refuse heaps broke the flatness, and where the narrow, shallowy Blackstaff River meandered, colourless and unmusical. Near its banks the tinkers camped. We at least held hopes in our heart—who knew, one day we might even have the chance of a council house. But the tinkers could not warm themselves with such a comfort but only over reluctant fires that hissed in the drizzle outside their tents of rags ...
>
> God ordained that even the Bog Meadows should end and had set a great hill at their limit, which we called the Mickeys' Mountain. In terms of miles the mountain was not far, and I always longed to explore it. Somewhere in the hidden hills behind, lay the boot stuffed with gold pieces buried by Neeshy Haughan, who, once upon a time, robbed the rich to pay the poor, kindnesses rewarded by a hanging at Carrickfergus. What things might be bought with the highwayman's long boot of gold! But the mountain was inaccessible because to reach it we had to cross territory held by the Mickeys. Being children of the staunch Protestant quarter, to go near the Catholic idolaters was more than we dared, for fear of having one of our members cut off. I settled early on rebel dreams. My father was too much like Neeshy Haughan, wild and free.

It was Shakespeare's enchanted wild wood but bigger, vast almost, stretching from the back doors of the residents, far south and west. The small strip of the Bog Meadows cringing alongside the motorway is all that is left today. Even so it is one of the richest centres of wildlife in Ireland.

Then, it was a wilderness of trees, rivers, lakes and the haunt of Romany Gypsies. Some of the Avenue dwellers became expert in the cultivation of health-giving herbs, many of which grew profusely in the Meadows. At 2/6d a doctor's visit, they were better value and, according to their most passionate advocates, a good deal more efficacious.

Robin Bryans roamed the meadows during the long summer days and evenings. He was befriended by the gypsies whom, he found, after some nervousness, were not interested in kidnapping Protestant boys for unknown, though undoubtedly sinister, purposes. Their lives seemed complete and generous in their poverty. And they taught him about the workings of nature and how to live off the land. The breadth of the land bounded only by the distant hills opened a mind in danger of being trapped by religiosity.

And yet it was certainly religion which offered him escape, not so much to future glory but by ameliorating the conditions of what was so often, with reason, adverted to as a vale of tears.

At the age of five, Robin Bryans had one of his most defining experiences. His father was, by profession, a window cleaner. Handsome, smiling, and full of a charm which was loved, though not entirely trusted, in the puritan world of Donegall Avenue. He was something of an artist and a gifted player on the melodeon with a voice of great sweetness. He was fond of good company and a glass or two, a predilection which did him no good at all with those of the neighbours who were monuments to a fairly stony sobriety.

Daily, whistling, Bryans senior would set off. Ladders balanced on his shoulders, buckets and shammies hanging on his arms, he would walk for miles to clean the windows of the better-off. There was an accident and Bryans fell from his balanced steps and crashed onto iron-spiked railings below.

His brain was irreparably damaged; his melodeon silenced for ever. The whistling and the singing stopped. The young Bryans watched him, trapped in his skull, the handsome young rover imprisoned for life by the kindness of neighbours and the watchful eye of the church:

> Then began the terrible days which have chased me down the long corridors of life ever since. For months he lay on the horsehair sofa in the kitchen, delirious in body and mind. I can see him now, unable to join us in the brass bed, lying amid bandages, and covered by his father's old lamplighter's greatcoat. He always wanted his melodeon near, though he could play it no longer ... Looking up, I saw tears rolling down the unshaven face. I thought maybe he was sorry for having filled the house with vast terror earlier in the day, when my mother went near to wash him. Or perhaps his soul was fighting to be out in the Bog Meadows with his red setter bitch, or playing his melodeon on the quayside as the emigrant boats sailed out from the harbour. Perhaps he wept because he realised that life was almost over, and he must leave the boys on the corner, the pigeons on the mangle in the backyard, the tin porringer of whelks from the Friday market and the little house in our row. And so it was.

At last he died. Now young Robin was a parish orphan of St. Simon's Church of Ireland. And he learned about music:

> The soul of music in our parish church, so far as I was concerned, lay within the great organ. I admired its ranks of pipes, the slim architecture of a heavenly city. After I discovered music its magnificence put everything else to shame. How I longed to master those white banks of stops, waiting like grapes in the harvest thanksgivings to be plucked by the handful; how my feet itched to flit over the obedient, throaty pedals, and my fingers to race over the tiered keyboards. But my enthusiasm was not enough to carry me far on the road to fame.
>
> —*No Surrender*

Music and uncultivated nature provide the staple imagery of his best work.

With his father dead, Robin's mother, the formidable Big 'Ina, had to work harder than ever. Long before dawn, the high heels of her shoes (Big 'Ina aspired to fashion, to the not unmixed approval of Presbyterian neighbours who felt that more attention to the next world would have suited her better) could be heard tapping down the length of the Avenue as she went on her rounds of cleaning the houses of the well-to-do. And it was a comedown about which her family had warned her. For Big 'Ina had married beneath her. That this was a fact could be and was affirmed by those members of her family who were still speaking to her. She could have done better than a melodeon-playing, drinking window cleaner, however handsome and charming. But, with harsh, ungenerous generosity, Christian charity was given whenever it was thought appropriate.

Cleaning provided the bread and butter of the family and Big 'Ina decided that a little jam from time to time would be nice. She began to take in lodgers. Mostly travellers or shipyard workers but, occasionally, musicians from visiting shows at the Opera House. Young Robin began to learn about the theatre. But there was still the question of his future to be decided.

One of the shipyard workers (opinion in the Avenue was divided concerning the regularity of his position in the Bryans household) got the boy an apprenticeship in Harland & Wolff. He became a cabin boy on a dredging ship in Belfast Harbour. It was a shock after the wild freedom of the Bog Meadows:

> We walked as though through a forest whose trees were made of steel, harshly etched against the morning sky. Instead of leaf-laden branches stretched out to catch the sun's rays, I saw a multitude of cranes, swinging poles and a phalanx of gantries ... On succeeding mornings I found the same people waiting for the same tram. Their complete submission to the harsh dictates of the shipyards faintly shocked me. Though friendly, the pale faces looked as if a light inside the men had long ago been extinguished. The men waiting for the tram seemed doomed to a gloomy world of metal, where no birds would sing nor brooks flow. And they accepted it. Standing behind each other, they were indistinguishable in their black clothes from

the man in front and the one behind.

—Up Spake the Cabin Boy

Harbinson's vivacity is, perhaps, his most distinguishing feature. During his life he has grasped the circumstances in which he found himself, shaken them vigorously and transmuted them into something else; something valuable, usually a book. His shipyard years formed the basis of his third volume of early autobiography, *Up Spake the Cabin Boy.*

For a boy with his gifts, imprisoned by class and poverty, in the 30s there was only one way out. Of course it was the church. Hellfire apart, the fundamentalist religions which abounded in the city were comparatively jolly. The music was both rousing and catchy compared with that of the Church of Ireland which tended towards musical gloom and liturgical rigidity. Then, too, there was undoubtedly something comfortable about being 'saved' when surrounded by the future damned. It might, perhaps, be that the exclusivity of the company of the 'saved,' and the irredeemable commonness of the (future) damned, added to conscious virtue that little extra spice needed to rescue it from insupportable dreariness and ease a little the terrible poverty of daily life.

Young Robin's constant endeavours to be good, shown by his regular appearances in the penitential pew, and his rises therefrom cleansed by the precious Blood of the Lamb, impressed his mentors and a place was secured for him at the Barry School of Evangelism in South Wales. Bryans' work was good, his examinations passed, and his apostolic future seemed secure.

So secure, that his first mission, possibly a thought ambitious, was to go to Canada and to convert the Indians there. But there was a hiatus. And Robin, with inspiration either divine or mundane, left the Indians unconverted, lived with them, learned from them and wrote the first of his excellent travel books.

His future, if not determined, was at least well signposted.

During the 60s and early 70s, his output was prolific. Published by Faber and acclaimed by English literary critics, came a series of travel books celebrating Ireland, Malta, Iceland, the Azores, Denmark and Brazil. They were more than just entertainment for armchair travellers. Bryans evoked the spirit of the places he wrote about, celebrated the living people.

In the same period came the four remarkable volumes of autobiography: *No Surrender*, *Song of Erne*, *Up Spake the Cabin Boy*, and *The Protégé*. Immediately they were recognised as being of exceptionally high quality. According to *The Times* he was 'on all planes at once; humorous, detailed and objective as a Bruegel village scene; quietly indignant over injustices ... He writes as one with a true sense of poetry'.

No Surrender was the first book by an Ulster Protestant writer from the working class published by an international publishing house to achieve national renown. It was a remarkable achievement; tough, tender, a pitilessly accurate and compelling look at Belfast working-class life in the 30s. Bryans' sharp observation, and his psychological insight, produced a work whose validity continues unencumbered by period or changes in economic circumstances. As in the work of Joseph Tomelty, the coherence of Bryans' worlds is not affected by time and place.

Belfast, more than any other city, has country connections. The great influx of country people at the end of the 19th century left behind their cousins, aunts and uncles and there are few Belfast citizens who have no relations in the country.

Donegall Avenue was the asphalt symbol of the rural/urban nature of the city. The residents on that side of the Avenue which backed onto the Bog Meadows were known for the variety of their livestock grazing in the meadows by day and at night securely locked up in the back yards. Ducks and chickens were too common to be mentioned; there were goats, pigs, cows, ponies and horses. When the circus visited Belfast even more exotic creatures made an appearance. And, further out across the meadows, their campfires shooting sparks high into the evening's boggy mists, were the gypsies. Their gaily coloured, painted caravans offering glimpses of a wilder, more romantic world than that which the staid, front doors of the houses gave onto.

Like Frank O'Connor, with whom he shares other qualities, Robert Harbinson's tone is a curious combination of the city and the country. And yet there is a difference. O'Connor's rural tone was formed by the small, constricted city of Cork, influenced by that city's isolated position in the south-west of Ireland, by its distance from Dublin and by O'Connor's intimate though strained relations with Dublin itself.

With Harbinson, the country and the city are almost the same. So closely intermeshed are they that it is difficult to separate one from the other. And so intriguing that much useless time is spent in trying to track down the precise literary form into which his voice neatly fits.

It doesn't. Harbinson's is an original voice. Part gypsy, part Belfast, his concern is the human condition viewed with an ironic eye and through a richly comic vision. The tone is, in fact, urbane. The urbanity, particularly in his early works, is often in extraordinary contrast with the grittiness of his subject matter forcing it, almost by stealth, on the reader.

In addition to the autobiographies, Harbinson's travels produced two volumes of excellent short stories: *Tattoo Lily* (1961) and *The Far World* (1962). The selection in this edition represents, to my mind, the best of his work.

'Tattoo Lily' is a joyous, rumbustious, dancing piece in which Harbinson's ironic vivacity is at its best. Only at the end of the comic narrative does a certain bleakness of vision allow itself to be felt. And even then you could very easily miss it out.

In 'The Hot Bed', he looks at middle-class puritanism and the Protestant ethos with clinical though sympathetic eyes. The world he creates here is a solid one, with all the comforts, the solidity of middle-class achievement. The initial cracks in the seemingly impregnable edifice, and the beginning of its disintegration, are superbly worked.

'Benedicite' concerns itself with the differences between appearance and reality, between shadow and substance, and of the unreality of the land of heart's desire. In it one is more inclined to notice similarities to O'Connor's best work. But

Harbinson's voice remains tough, northern. One notices the resemblances and dismisses them as irrelevant.

'L'Après-Midi d'un Faune' is especially good. Yet it is so simple. A day in the life of a 13-year-old boy, its denouement is his first orgasm and its result on his life. It is a simple but exquisite sharing of a rite of passage.

It is true that Robert Harbinson was the first working-class Protestant writer whose work was criticised at a national level and, perhaps, whose readership was greater abroad than at home but it would be wrong to say that his was the voice of a class. Or of Protestantism, though there is no doubt that the cast of his mind is Protestant. His stubbornness, for example. His refusal to stay the cosy Irish pet of the establishment and his later, dramatic forays into the more obscure byways of British politics, all mark him out as a rebel.

While I admire his integrity, I regret that his subject matter changed. His last three books, published by Honeyford Press, *The Dust Has Never Settled, Let the Petals Fall* and *Checkmate* are written with his usual verve and are full of fascinating information. As far as Northern Ireland is concerned, they are also filled with riveting, often scandalous, detail and should be required reading for anyone interested in the underbelly of Unionism.

But to me the regrets remain. In the early autobiographies the young Robin Bryans wandered the Belfast streets and gave to the rivers of the Bog Meadows the same local habitation and name that Tom Sawyer gave to the mud banks of the Mississippi. The boy Robin and the writer Robin Bryans were at once the same and yet different. The man understood and loved the boy and the boy would clearly become the man; but not quite yet.

Robert Harbinson lives in London where he is closely involved in a school of music set up particularly to encourage the work of young composers.

John Keyes
25th December 1995

Benedicite

FOR FORTY YEARS MISS SKELLY HAD dreamed of a cottage in the Antrim Glens. Even during her maiden voyage to India as a young missionary, the dream of a whitewashed cottage among her native hills had torn her heart to shreds. For one dreadful moment before the ship's gangway was taken away from Ulster soil she had been tempted to fly down it leaving luggage and all behind. But she recalled the bitter remorse suffered by St. Peter when he denied his Lord, so she had manned the rail and watched the coastline drop below the horizon. Miss Skelly was a woman with inexhaustible powers of dedication called to minister to India's millions, to their bodies and souls, and from the outset she determined not to allow homesickness to interfere with her work. When your hand is on the plough, she always told herself, you don't look back. But the very mention of the word 'plough' brought to her mind scenes of rich turned earth, soft skies, and the noble profile of Antrim.

At first she had tried complete denial and lived in the mission compound like an ascetic. The resultant torture, however, proved to be more of a stumbling block than the occasional bouts of homesickness which her pictures might bring. So she

got them out of the trunks and hung them about her rooms.
There were views of Antrim valleys and Antrim hills and sad
watercolours of lonely coasts. In each a cottage could be seen,
white against a background of blue distance. A painting showing
the soup-plate hump of Slemish held the principal place in this
private collection. It gave Miss Skelly at once her proudest and
tenderest memories. On this mountain where St. Patrick had
herded Milchu's swine and filled his young soul with missionary
vision, Miss Skelly had given her life to the Muslims of India.
Sitting amongst the mountain's heather she had studied her first
Urdu characters. Compared with some, her missionary society
had been generous in the amount of furlough, and when
returning from each leave she took more and more *bric-à-brac*
back to the sub-continent. They were tiny links in the chain
that bound her to home. She had even made a miniature stack
of turves, bringing a few peats each time from the beloved
moors. But they were not for fires because sinister dust-devils
often besieged the mission, tall columns of soil and sand that
raced across the burning plains like tiny tornados. The heat had
been a greater enemy to Miss Skelly than any temptations from
the Evil One.

For the past ten years, however, Miss Skelly had not seen
Ulster. The war made furlough impossible. When that was over
there were the upheavals of partition into India and Pakistan,
and the consequent uncertainty as to whether the mission would
be allowed to stay at all. Naturally in such times as these you
stuck to your post of duty. And then, it seemed in no time at all
Miss Skelly was crossing vast parched wastes of the Sindi desert
and was sailing from Karachi for the last time. Such an air of
finality settled on this journey, as dust settled in the railway
carriage. Miss Skelly knew that she was leaving India and the
new Pakistan for ever. At least she could feel happy that her
beloved people had achieved Iqbal's vision of the 'pure land'
even though the Lord had not converted them. Their bright
future would blush, as it were, unseen in the desert, for Miss
Skelly would not be there. She was old and ailing, and her life's

work done. But at last (was it possible?) she was going to the dream cottage. The simple life which seemed the Lord's reward for all the selfless years of service in His vineyard would soon be hers. There would be no more New Testaments in Pushtu to pack for the Khyber traveller, no more escaping to the hill stations nor conventions at Murree.

Within a month Miss Skelly's trunks and cases were landed at Belfast and she walked down the gangway as forty years previously she had walked up it. Where had the forty years gone? Now that were over they seemed only like a few months. Miss Skelly certainly could not believe that a whole decade had slipped by since her last visit to the city of ships and Protestant zeal. At first sight she could see no changes in the welcome skyline of roofs and turrets and domes, except perhaps in the shipyards where the gantries seemed denser than she remembered. But Queen's Bridge was still there with busy people hurrying across it like lemmings. When she emerged from the Customs Shed, Miss Skelly noticed that there were no trams any more. Fear and disappointment laid a finger on her heart

All the way from Karachi, through the swelter of the Red Sea, over the ethereal blue of the Mediterranean, under the shadow of the Rock, up through the muddy Bay of Biscay, Miss Skelly had played a game with herself. It consisted of enjoying in anticipation the thrill to be experienced on getting her first tram. She specially arranged her luggage so that there was nothing to carry except a valise filled with last minute purchases from the trading boys of Port Said who had swarmed the liner. With this bag she had proposed climbing on to the top of the tram and seeing the sights before going to the station. Miss Skelly knew the number of the trams she must get and the amount of the fare. The tram smell and the hissing wheels on rails filled her imagination. Several times on board ship she had gone up the gangway between one deck and another, pretending that it was the tram stairs. She had muttered to an imaginary conductor at the bottom that he if wished she would pay her fare now and save him at least *one* journey. 'I've just come back from the East you know,' she had planned to whisper confidentially in his ear as the tram lurched forward. Some passengers on board ship had caught her at this game and came to the conclusion that the old lady was definitely gaga, running up and down like that, talking to herself. But Miss Skelly had merely smiled sweetly at them—after all *they* had no idea what lay behind her behaviour. And now there were no trams.

The Albert struck the hour and Miss Skelly tried to get a taxi. Even her beloved Ulster was becoming modernised, not excluding the Belfast people's manners. The way some of them jumped the queue and bundled in the taxis that drew up, because they were younger and quicker than Miss Skelly, was quite outrageous. She found it most unworthy too of such a Christian capital as Belfast. To conceal from herself a growing apprehension as to what other losses and changes she was about to discover, Miss Skelly allowed herself a little righteous anger which burst from her as 'Really!' and 'Excuse me, but I was ... ' In the end she let out a breath, half sigh, half sob. For a moment the crowd of loving faces that had seen her off in Pakistan had come unbidden into her mind. How different their warmth was from the hostility of her own people, where not a soul had come to welcome her home. When a taxi-driver did take notice of her he grumbled about the small amount she tipped him. How could this coarse man, she thought, understand that those living on faith in the mission field even nowadays received no more than a hundred pounds in the year? Everything was awkward, difficult, frustrating, expensive. The city had become foreign to her. Luggage difficulties repeated themselves at the station and once again Miss Skelly's thoughts flew back to Sammy, the mission's camel with oily black sides like *lederhosen*, who had pulled the boxes to the station with such dignified steps.

Once in the train and well away from the unpleasantness in the horrid capital, Miss Skelly recovered. She asked forgiveness for her indulgence in self-pity, a sin she regarded as practically unforgivable. During a long life in the East she had witnessed so much suffering, seen so many people die of hunger and disease, that she had vowed never to complain about anything that might happen to her. With thankful heart Miss Skelly knew she was going towards rest and peace in the glens of her childhood, the moorland home of her questing spirit, and the rugged shores of the sand-pickers. With infinite joy she saw the well-loved landscape forming around the train. Her heart leapt as landmarks she had forgotten came into view—a hill shoulder there, a farm by a river, and wayside stations whose names were poetry. So with a great deal of fussing and hissing the train pulled into the market town. And there to crown the wanderer's return was a splendid sight which reduced Miss Skelly to tears. By pressing against the glass she had seen what they had all done to welcome her back from a life's labour in the Lord's service. On the platform stood a grand welcoming committee, and behind them Miss Skelly caught a glimpse of the town's brass band. The eyes that looked into the mirror were moist, and Miss Skelly found it difficult to make sure that her grey locks were firmly caged under the elastic of her straw hat. In case they asked her to make a speech when she stepped from the train, Miss Skelly slipped a pocket Testament into the coat she was wearing, so that an appropriate word of scripture might be to hand.

Although the train crept into the station at a pace no faster than a snail's, it stopped with an almighty jolt which threw Miss Skelly off balance. It also interrupted her thoughts as to how she would address the committee. Should it be 'Dear Brethren in the Lord' or simply 'Friends'? Being not entirely without a sense of drama, Miss Skelly considered the greatest impact would be made if she sat on and let them burst into the compartment. This would have the added advantage that they could then manage her luggage too. By now the engine noise had subsided to a whisper of escaping steam. The blissful strains of 'Home Sweet Home' as rendered by the band seemed to Miss Skelly the most beautiful music she had ever heard. And it was not until she had wiped her glasses for the second time that Miss Skelly realised that the music was retreating down the platform and out into the station yard. The banging of carriage doors told her that the train was about to move on. She shouted from the window, and the guard stopped the train in time. Apart from him the platform was empty. Confused and upset Miss Skelly got her boxes out. Eyes brimming and lip quivering the old lady then noticed four of her old friends at the barrier. She was so pleased that she failed to notice how much older, more lined and sadder they all looked. Miss Skelly tried to be brave when they told her that the welcoming committee and band had not been for her at all, but for a young Satanite who had been to some international sports abroad and won a silver medal in hop, step and jump.

In their sincere expression of joy for her safe return from foreign parts, however, her friends more than compensated for the disappointment. Miss Skelly realised she had been vain and proud and full of self-pity again. Her skill in diagnosing particular forms of the Evil One's attacks was one quality not diminished by advancing years. Any canker within herself was dealt with immediately. But what could she do about the wickedness without? Miss Skelly observed that it invaded even her own home-town. Her friends drove her in an old motor-car home to tea, and she could see many changes. When she voiced her disapproval, the friends said that worse than the things which could be seen, were those that could not. For instance, the rector allowed dancing at the church-hall socials, and the squire had divorced his poor arthritic wife to marry a painted Jezebel from the city, and she, of all things, was said to have once been an actress. Then the car turned into the High Street and Miss Skelly got the biggest shock of all. There was the fine Georgian house that used to be her Uncle Willie's home. Now it stood desecrated for all to see, transformed into a sinner's nest. Godless women sat brazenly in the front parlour windows reading magazines while their permanently-waved hair dried under plastic beehives. Now Miss Skelly did give way to her tears. What hours of prayer and praise had echoed through the High Street from that very room, a place that had been sacred for many generations, ever since John Wesley had preached in it while on his farmhouse mission to Ulster.

Miss Skelly's first night in Ireland was to be spent with the local prayer-secretary of her mission society. This woman was also deaconess at a church in the town. Though growing older like her missionary friend, the deaconess was still giving fine witness on the new housing estate. Miss Skelly, however, was too excited to take in all the soul-winning news and excused herself for bed. But she could not sleep and lay staring at the square of window waiting for it to lighten with the dawn, and herald her last lap to the cottage.

One of the things for which she felt most grateful was that a cottage had been got for her already, and indeed its new paint was still wet. It could boast of nothing and had been a humble shepherd's affair. When the ancient man died, Miss Skelly had wired the first and only cable in her life, arranging with a friend to make an offer for the cottage. Soon she would be living out on the moors along with God's own creatures and the pure wind of the wide oceans. What a wonderful end to her days, where she could close her door on the world, snug inside the thick walls, that under their guardian elms were the true Hebron of her dreams. Indeed, the excitement of achieving her heart's desire made Miss Skelly think of the young bride Achsah being offered the upper and nether springs of Hebron. Miss Skelly felt certain that her cottage was a place of fellowship with God, the land of living water and streams of spiritual refreshment flowing through the unspoilt pastures of Antrim. Nothing could be plainer than that this was the Lord's reward to her for those long years in the wilderness.

As early in the morning as was decently possible, she left the town and made her way to the country. A tractor had already taken the luggage. Miss Skelly tactfully avoided the help of friends who wanted to go with her and assist in arranging the furniture that had been laid in store since her mother's death. To be entirely alone at her long dreamt-of homecoming was essential to Miss Skelly, now that it was actually happening. Forty years of anticipation could not be spoilt by others' chatter, however well-meaning. Even as a little girl she had left her brothers and sisters to climb hedges and hills, so that she could play at keeping house by herself in a disused corbelled pigsty.

She got a carter to take her up to the cottage which proved to be more beautiful than ever she had expected or remembered. The excitement flustered her so that she dropped things and could not find others that were right under her nose. At last she took control of herself and determined to tackle one problem at a time. She hummed a Gospel chorus that had been a favourite with her Punjabi people and plied her needle to the adjustment of some curtains. The material was rough and woven with a pattern of red and green stripes on a white background, typical in fact of the material woven by Punjabi women within the confines of purdah. These particular lengths of the material reminded her of the old carpet-seller who had sat every day by the mission gates, shaving his legs and armpits until a customer came along. The lengths of curtain had been brought from him years ago and packed away against this very day. And they were still as good as new, perhaps better than she remembered now they were actually in the Antrim light. And what glorious, heavenly light of a September morning it was, shining and serene. Miss Skelly rejoiced and looked from her tiny windows on to the splendid landscape around her, pure, mellow, haunted by plovers, enriched with bilberries.

The interior decoration could not be completed at once because the paint on the walls had still to dry. The walls were of the palest of greys and this was lucky for on the sitting-room walls she intended to hang her Turkoman Tent-bag and her prayer-rug from Bokhara. The light grey would show up the lustrous sheen, the ancient soft pile, the diapason of dyes and textures, the stately gardens and streams of eternity that wreathed richly on her carpet hangings. Miss Skelly had brought enough oriental rugs and camel-bag besides *durris* woven by the mission women from their own sheep, back to Ireland to cover every wall and floor in the whole cottage. But whether she would do this or only have a few up at a time and change them periodically would be something to think about during the coming weeks. All her life Miss Skelly had been a hard worker, never resting until the job was complete. She neglected food, neglected letters to her friends, except for one of great length to the mission, telling with praise of all her journeying mercies. Miss Skelly slaved until the cottage was 'shipshape and true' as she liked to describe a task well done. When she sat back and surveyed her handiwork, the trim neatness of it all, she knew that her happiness was replete.

Now she could turn her eyes unto the hills, especially the hill which towered above the cottage and which was hers all except for a handful of silent ewes. One afternoon in the second week Miss Skelly locked the cottage and dropped the key into her new leather shoulder bag bought at Port Said and tooled with a view of the pyramids of Gizah. Miss Skelly also carried her lunch of home-made griddled scones and cheese for she planned to conquer the highest peak. On top of the lunch packets rested her pocket Testament where a hand could easily reach it. Not since she had gone to the hill station at Nathiagali at the foot of the Himalayas four years previously had Miss Skelly done so much climbing. Shortly she was out of breath and wondered if she would ever make the top. By resting and lightening her shoulder-bag by eating, she came gradually to the heights and finally to the cloud-dappled panorama of Antrim. Not far away, shining like silver filigree, was the sea. But Miss Skelly turned her back on that. It was still painful for her to think that the sea ran unbroken all the way to Karachi. So she studied the noble landscape instead.

Elevated places in which to sit had always excited her. She gave vent to her feelings of exultation by means of the *Benedicite*. Whenever she contemplated the wonders of creation seen in concert together the canticle came to her lips. But it seldom corresponded liturgically to that *Benedicite* which can be found in the order for Morning Prayer. Miss Skelly's canticle was not in fact to be found in *any* book. She took her cue from Bishop Taylor Smith whom she had once heard in the big tent at the Keswick convention. He explained how once he had walked in the gardens at Oxford and addressed the flowers, '*O all ye delphiniums, bless ye the Lord: praise him, and magnify him for ever.*' Since that day Miss Skelly had never hesitated to improvise upon the theme wherever she might be, whether walking through the pine wood at Murree towards Lawrence College, or breathing the crisp air among the alpine splendours of Nathiagali. But wherever her *Benedicite* had been uttered she always remembered Ulster: '*O all ye orange lilies and thundering Lambeggers, bless ye the Lord: praise him and magnify him for ever.*'

Gratefully, joyfully, Miss Skelly sank into the soft bed of heather on the mountain's flank. When a little strength returned she straightened her back and began to sing. All the same, it did not seem odd that her *Benedicite* was not of Ulster and its beauties, not of the green land that had haunted all her years in the heat of the Punjab plains, but of those very plains themselves. Her tone rang clear and strong so she failed to detect in it a marked nostalgia:

> *O ye spreading pipal trees, bless ye the Lord:*
> *praise him, and magnify him for ever.*
> *O ye bobbed-haired dancing boys, bless ye the Lord:*
> *praise him, and magnify him for ever.*
> *O ye Tajiks and Persian traders of the sharbet booths, bless ye*
> *the Lord:*
>> *Praise Him, and magnify Him for ever.*
>> *O ye tribal lads and hairy Sikhs, bless ye the Lord:*
>> *Praise Him, and magnify Him for ever.*
>> *O let Pakistan bless the Lord:*
>> *Praise Him, and magnify Him for ever.*

When Miss Skelly finished she was surprised not only to find herself standing up, but also that her eyes were wet.

However, Miss Skelly did not intend to forget *The glamour of thy footsteps in the north* and on the very next night had planned her house-warming. All remaining friends and relatives had been invited out from the town. Miss Skelly was going to surprise and please them with an Eastern repast. That night she went to bed early, heavily but pleasantly tired with her climbing, and was up early in the morning to prepare her feast. But the feast had taken years to prepare, years of patient learning from her Punjabi women. Miss Skelly's arms ached beyond endurance by the time she had finished beating the silver sheet to a diaphragm hardly more substantial than breath in frosty air. When laid and folded gently over the pudding this precious flake of silver looked as lavish and extravagant as she hoped her guests would expect of oriental food. The silver coating was supposed to strengthen the heart and she would tell them so—though she was not trying to charm the heart of the old Army Scripture Reader as the Queen of Sheba had presumably done when serving her sweetmeats in silver to Solomon.

Miss Skelly worked so hard preparing the feast that she barely had time to dress herself before the first guests arrived. Apart from the transformation their hostess had effected on the cottage, giving it quite an oriental flavour with rugs and carpets, there was the table. She had put a whole month's allowance into the meal. The stiff table linen was crowded with dishes and graced by the slender necked *aftabas* full of spring water. Everyone agreed that these silver ewers gave the final touch of Eastern splendour. Beaming Miss Skelly bade her guests sit down. When they began to eat the strange concoctions their pleasure visibly wilted. For soup there was a sumptuous *kalla paincha*, but on stirring hers and seeing a sheep's eye looking at her the prayer-secretary nearly fainted. This created a stir from which the party never recovered. Out of sheer kind politeness, the others toyed with odd pieces, but Miss Skelly's sharp eye observed that apart from nibbling harmless *chappatis*, hardly a thing was eaten. Things barely brightened when the evening finished with green tea. But after chatting and singing a few choruses to the accompaniment of the small collapsible harmonium Miss Skelly had used at the mission, they all began with one consent to make excuses, and by ten o'clock had gone.

A curious thought then came to Miss Skelly. Looking back afterwards she recognised that the beginning of the end, as it were, could be dated from it. After closing the gate behind the last departed visitor she went inside the house again and surveyed the room and the remains. How odd, how very odd, she said aloud several times. For what she had once done to her rooms in the mission compound, she had now been doing to her dream cottage, only in reverse. Forty years ago she had done everything possible to make the mission look like a little bit of Antrim. In the bazaar she could never reckon except in pounds and shillings. But now, here she was doing her best to make the cottage as Pakistani as she could, even in the way she entertained her friends. Only outside did the house resemble the white cottage in the hills that had lured her and helped her through an arduous life in the field. In fact, on recalling her dream of the delectable mountains and the white cottage, Miss Skelly realised that she had always thought of it from the outside. In the wanderings and walks she had planned, she had always been approaching the cottage, or walking away from it, or gazing down on it from an Antrim hilltop. But apart from sitting snugly by the turf fire with roaring gales outside, she had never conceived of herself being in it. And she had not, in fact, had the idea of hanging her rugs and camel-bags and the placing of her fine Peshawari metalwork until the last few days on the voyage. While putting them up, while preparing her feast, Miss Skelly knew that uppermost in her mind was not the homecoming to Antrim, but the faraway mission and her smiling Pakistanis. They were constantly in her mind. Everyday she stopped to look at her watch and say, 'Now if I was *there* I should be opening the dispensary.' Most peculiar of all was that she calculated her monthly allowance and the price of the groceries out from the town in rupees and annas.

Depressed, Miss Skelly sat by the fire. The pile of plates and cutlery waiting to be washed seemed malevolent. And there was not enough water left in the house to wash them. She could not push open a wire fly-screen door and call a water-carrier nor call even the meanest of sweeper-boys to come and tidy the room. She would have to do it herself, and in the morning she would have to make another journey to the well. For nearly half a century Miss Skelly had been waited on hand and foot, served by her own bearer and received all the other attentions that befitted a white woman under the shadow of the Union Jack. Miss Skelly did not think that to do such tasks in her cottage would be to demean herself, for she believed and taught that the Lord could be glorified in the humblest of duties. Yet it was hard to change a whole way of life just when peace and stillness and rest had appeared to be just within reach. But beyond reach were the ordinary blessings of life, even a bath. Miss Skelly would have fled from the cottage. But there was no refuge where the patter of the bearers' bare feet over the tiles could be heard as the men filled the old mission bathtub, and where she could see the fat yellow lizards clinging to the ceiling to catch flies. Taking an oil lamp Miss Skelly went into the bedroom knowing she would never have a proper bath at the cottage. Then she cried herself to sleep.

But fresh and salty Antrim mornings are medicine for any ills of the heart. Miss Skelly woke late with the sun bright and clear. She set to at once, fetched her water and long before midday had removed every sign of the feast from both the cottage and her own mind. A wariness possessed her now, however, and she was cautious in her love for the cottage. When she looked from the windows at the hills she checked the flow of poetic thoughts that had rushed unfailing through her mind before. From those hills would come the winds and storms that would double the work of keeping warm and the long dreary days of rain that would mean a soaking to the skin every time she went to the well. And so, of course, it came to be. Summer died slowly, but Miss Skelly noted with misgiving how the sun's heat grew uncertain and how it set earlier and more angrily. Mornings were tart with autumn and long trails of mist hung eerily about hollows in the valleys. Her friends no longer came so frequently to see her and sit on the bit of lawn by the roses to gossip and drink tea. Instead they sent short notes saying how difficult the mountain roads were in the rain but of course dear Miss Skelly was always more than welcome whenever she went into the town.

This isolation wounded Miss Skelly, for though it had been part of her dream, she had always imagined that her retirement would be filled with loving fellowship just whenever she wished. But now the difficult winter days locked her in a windy prison. Bitter cold set in by January and Miss Skelly kept the fire in day and night. She had forgotten the old skill of banking up the turf fire to make it last through the night, so she was often up stocking and stacking. She had never known such cold before, not even up at Nathiagali where Himalayan winds brought snow and frosts to the pine-clad slopes. She supposed that the tropics had thinned her blood. With the same courage that had sent her to the mission field Miss Skelly faced the winter's onslaught. For ten days she was snowed in and not a human soul came near. When the thaw came the roof began to leak in a dozen places so she had to set buckets and jars to catch the falling stalactites of water. The drip, drip, drip sounded like whispering voices and played on her nerves. As soon as the roads were clear Miss Skelly went into town and bought a dog. Living so far away from help Miss Skelly had decided that a dog was necessary to warn of approaching strangers, though being strong in the fear of the Lord she was no coward.

Again she was snowed in and although the patter of the dog's feet at night was a comfort, Miss Skelly faced the days ahead until the thaw with dread. In the midst of the fever of life and work in the mission she had often paused to think wistfully and longingly of such a situation. When the fiercest Indian summer sun and hot dry winds had scorched the very air she breathed, snow and snow-covered hills and crackling fire, and hot tea and toast had meant more to her than Paradise itself. After Partition the mission compound was filled with hopeless, homeless refugees who squatted in hundreds about the place, waiting patiently like animals to be fed, clothed and housed. As Miss Skelly walked out of her house they followed her with their eyes dumbly begging for things she could not give them. Compassion filled her, pity ruled her heart. But there were times when Miss Skelly cried to the Lord to give her rest and relief if only for a

week or so—no *Benedicites* then, only the psalmist's longing for
the wings of a dove. In Antrim now her prayers were answered
with a vengeance, for not even the deaf postman came near the
place. Not since girlhood when she played alone in the old
pigsty had Miss Skelly been so alone.

Memories of girlhood showed Miss Skelly all too clearly that
she had not faced so many fundamental probings of her soul
since the day she wrestled with the Lord on Slemish and finally
surrendered to His call. As she sat in the silent cottage watching
the dog worrying her precious Kirman saddle-cover to shreds,
Miss Skelly peered deep into her innermost being. Could it be
that the Lord was using this as a testing time and that greater
things than ever before lay in store? Then she would be filled
with remorse for such dour ungratefulness. Such were the fancies
of the lonely woman who could not hide from herself the fact
that what she had wanted for so long, and on first achieving had
loved, was now bitter and hateful. She began to neglect the
cottage, and let dust collect on the fringes of her hanging
carpets, and did not polish the metalwork, so that it grew dull
and lifeless. The cold seemed to be in her bones and she stayed
in bed nearly all day in the worst weather.

But Miss Skelly was not idle. In her blue fingers she held the
pocket Testament, and as always when distressed she searched
its pages for comfort and strength. At that time her daily portion
of scriptures was taken from the Pentateuch which had always
been her favourite books. Her thoughts lingered over the
Pharaoh's dreams. The ill favoured and lean-fleshed kine
coming out of the river to devour the well favoured and fat-
fleshed kine seemed so like her own life. The years on the hot
plains and by the North-West Frontier had swallowed her youth
and womanhood whole, leaving her quite incapable of settling
in the bracing winds of Antrim. She had always been too busy to
stop and think about herself too much and to observe how every
hour on the sub-continent was changing her and making the
dream life of retirement an impossibility. When winter began to
ebb, and the last snows disappeared and tiny swellings that

would become buds were seen on twigs once more, Miss Skelly's mind was made up. Quite definitely the cottage was not the Lord's will. In the practical way that she always treated God, Miss Skelly left the next move to Him.

As soon as spring was well in, she set out for Slemish to re-dedicate herself, and beg forgiveness for the self-centredness that had led her from the true path of duty. Lord deliver me, she cried, but recognising at the same time that this was rather a tall order, for as far as she could tell, she was quite unable to do anything but stay put at the cottage. All her savings had gone into buying the little place and nothing could be done on her minute allowance. Nevertheless, she had faith and by the end of the week she had a token of the Lord's forgiveness.

The deaf postman handed her a letter with a London postmark. The spidery handwriting was familiar yet she could not place it exactly. From the importance letters played in the old days in India (she was always calling them the old days) Miss Skelly had devised a means of making the pleasure of their arrival last longer. This was to postpone slitting the envelopes until she guessed the sender's identity from the handwriting,. For this reason she had deplored the introduction of typewriters and had always asked her friends not to use them. Miss Skelly shouted thanks at the postman, which he did not hear, and took the letter to the fireside. She tapped it on her knee, held it up to the light but could not guess. The writing was not by any of the few lady friends she had who lived in London. Strangely, she would have expected that sort of writing from pupils at her mission school. Defeated but delighted she inserted the point of a paper-knife and opened the envelope. No longer able to bear the suspense she turned the sheet of notepaper over and read the signature. There were two—Abdul and Khalid.

A flush of pleasure reddened her face. Of course, how stupid of her to have forgotten those two delightful boys on the ship who shared much of her journey home! Miss Skelly had spent a lot of time with them trying to improve their English as they were going to London to study engineering. When younger, the

boys had been pupils at the mission school. There had been
times when they were so lively and full of untrammelled energy
that they threatened to wreck the mission's quiet discipline. But
Miss Skelly had always been specially fond of them. Had she
ever had children of her own she would have wanted two exactly
like the mischievous Abdul and Khalid.

Miss Skelly was excited because the boys had not forgotten
her, and she read the letter through without taking in a single
thing it said. Then she made a cup of tea and settled down. It
was difficult to read, of course, because the boys' English
grammar was bad and their spelling worse. But then it had
always been. Gradually it dawned on Miss Skelly that the boys
were asking if they might come to Ireland and visit her. Their
winter too had been bad both with studies and health. Abdul
particularly had been ill with a cough and now both of them
wanted to stay in the green Irish countryside during the Easter
vacation to recuperate. When she digested it all Miss Skelly
immediately sat at her desk and replied, bidding the brothers
come at once. Then she sang choruses in Urdu and dashed about
the cottage cleaning and brightening, and had the Punjabi
curtains washed and flying in the wind like flags. On board ship
when she had given the young students her address, Miss Skelly
had not believed they would ever bother about her. The boys
had gone through the mission school and yet had not come out
on the Lord's side, and even now they were still devout Muslims.
Nevertheless Miss Skelly felt sure that the Lord's hand was in
this thing and wonderful works were prepared for her to do.

Easter came bringing Abdul and Khalid. Miss Skelly went to
meet them at the station and they embraced, she with tears. As
they rocked up the rutted roads the boys skylarked and sang and
frightened the horse, and when they saw the cottage said it was
just like home which, of course, with all its Indian *bric-à-brac*, it
was. Miss Skelly's happiness overflowed now that she once more
had someone to appreciate her curries and *chappatis*, carry her
water, sing to her in subtle quarter-tones, and wear the gleaming
white *shalwars* to bring back the lost years. In her letter she had

insisted that they bring their baggy cotton trousers and behave just as they would in Pakistan. Abdul and Khalid needed no encouragement and the silent cottage was noisy and full of laughter. Even the dog stopped biting the carpets. It went for such long walks over the hills with the boys in the evenings it just lay exhausted by the fire, following every move with soulful eyes and occasional throbs at the end of a straggly tail.

And then the four blissful weeks were over and they were all down at the station again, the boys in staid suits and Miss Skelly with another flow of tears. The only twinge of conscience felt by Abdul and Khalid was that they had done no studying, and by Miss Skelly that she had not helped them by speaking Urdu instead of English.

The future, however, was far from gloomy, for in eight weeks they promised to return and stay with their old missionary teacher during the long summer vacation. Miss Skelly's days were filled with radiant life. The winter rigours lay forgotten as the beauty of Antrim blossomed again. Birds came back to their familiar haunts and in every crevice surprising, nameless wild flowers sprang up. Miss Skelly pondered on the turn of events. Had the Lord brought these two young men all the way from the East in order that she might be instrumental in saving their Muslim souls? It seemed most likely, although she never discussed religion for she was afraid that a broadside attack would scare them away.

By June Miss Skelly was busy making her jams and pickles in preparation for a more cheerful winter. Then came another letter from London. Abdul and Khalid had fared badly in their studies and could not sit the examinations, so they were working in restaurants. Unfortunately they would not be able to come over to Ireland as planned. No more picnics up on the moors, they wrote with bland cheerfulness.

This so upset Miss Skelly that she put the letter down unfinished and wept bitterly. When the paroxysm passed she read on and found sorrow turned to joy. If only they could lay their hands on a few hundred pounds the boys had a wonderful chance of opening an Indian restaurant of their own, though, wrote Khalid in his engaging frankness, this would only be a success if they had someone really experienced like Miss Skelly to cook for them. No doubt remained in Miss Skelly's mind as to where the Lord was leading. Even at the end of her life, He had given her work for Him, even given her the special skills required for its doing, since she knew a least a hundred dishes which would make the London business a flourishing success. The sale of the old, damp cottage would easily fetch the necessary capital and what a setting her carpets and camel-bags would provide. Naturally, the restaurant being Muslim and Christian would not be licensed, and a prayer would go out with every plate of curry.

Miss Skelly's farewells with her friends in the town were brief. The prayer-secretary thought she was mad and said so. But then the prayer-secretary did not know how delicious a properly cooked sheep's eye can be, or how refreshing the fragrant green tea of the shabet booths really is.

Praise flowed from Miss Skelly during the whole journey. London loomed before her a visionary city, and yet the greatest vineyard that needed dressing. Crossing the water, and on the long train journey she sang a new canticle, the finest *Benedicite* she had ever sung.

O ye smogs and chilly evenings, bless ye the Lord:
   Praise Him, and magnify Him for ever.
O ye green parks and flowing Thames, bless ye the Lord:
   Praise Him, and magnify Him for ever.
O let Piccadilly and Leicester Square bless the Lord:
   Praise Him, and magnify Him for ever.

Quality Tea

UNLESS YOU HAD A GOAT IN season nobody would ever dream of going down the old bog road. The cutting of its turf banks had been begun long ago, much longer ago than any living memory. Now they were all cut away and sally bushes sprung up with such riotous living that half the ploughland looked like primeval scrub, as though no man from the dawn of time had ever walked there. The place had a weird, deserted air, not least because it was dangerous. Neither the people round about, nor any of their beasts ever strayed among the smiling, treacherous, sally aisles, for they were no more than a camouflage for deep, silent bogholes. Even the Sunday courting couples never took a turn amongst the heather any more on their way home from the Preaching House. And that was condemnation of the old bog road indeed.

Nevertheless, when the mating call came to every goat of the barony, the narrow path through the bog led to Aggie Cerson's billy. Aggie lived at the end of the long lane, shut off from the world by a screen of sallies that hid her three-roomed cottage. Though Aggie was old she was not so old as her cottage. Like her, it had a good thatch to it. But whereas age had turned

Aggie's to silver, all it had done to the cottage's was to plant a spattering of bright green mossy hummocks here and there on the weather-beaten straw. The walls beneath it, crumbling, uneven walls that leaned inwards, were always impeccably white, and this was Aggie's own handiwork. Despite her more-than-seventy years Aggie still managed to give the walls a good yearly dressing of whitewash inside and out before the swallows returned to their old haunts in the byre.

Since her brother had died none of the stake chains in the byre had graced a cow's neck, though Aggie still carried out of the dim shed enough dung to plant her Kerr's Pinks which would last the house and a hundred head of fowl for a year. Aggie could not complain about the treatment her neighbour gave her and she had at least three dropped calves, and maybe a couple of pet pigs come her way for all the lush grass and surplus milk of the three goats. What with the sale of these at the spring fairs, her eggs, and the fees for her billy, Aggie lived, as she herself described it, like castle-folk. And, had she chosen, Aggie could have lived even better, but she did not choose. That would have entailed going down three miles of the new council road to tell the bold hussy in the grocer's post office her age in order that Aggie might draw the old-age pension. Like any duchess, Aggie had her pride. In any case, although the creamery lorry no longer called at the top of the lane, she still had the grass for four cows and was mortally afraid that a pension application would bring the inspectors prowling round. Not indeed that she did not keep the fields in good order.

With every summer that came round she still had as many rucks of hay to win, as in the farm's heyday when her brother cut for the whole neighbourhood with his two Clydesdales. And if the rheumatism gripping her with its cruel talons should cause her to hang up the scythe in the dark barn for ever, Aggie had an answer for that. She had enough paper money laid by to get the cheeky young skite from the crossroads to come down with his fancy mowing machine. Paper money was good enough for him, although in her heart Aggie held such money in great contempt and never felt that she got proper value when the van-man paid her proceeds from the egg sales once a week. The van-man had long grown accustomed to her distrustful look as he counted the notes into her hand. He merely thought she suspected *him* of cheating, not the Bank of England itself. Whenever possible Aggie persuaded him to give silver. The mice and rats in the thatch would have more difficulty in nibbling at the coins' milled edges than the crumpled, worthless-looking banknotes.

Aggie was no fool and had built a dyke against any seas of infirmity which might batter her. The dread workhouse would never swallow her, Aggie had decided, and to this end she kept secret her possession of a tea-caddy, with pictures on its sides of Queen Victoria and Balmoral Castle. None but she knew that it was hid under the turf stack. More than a hundred golden sovereigns rattled in that tea-caddy. The clink of it was heavenly to hear. Yet Aggie had been unable to add to the golden pile since she had placed the two from her brother's watch-chain on top, five years previously.

When the bog had been in full use with forty banks or more sliced away, it could keep as many families in fuel for a year. From the damp, compressed layers of buried fenland and forests were quarried the strangely-yielding stones destined for an architecture of flame, smoke and soft white ash. But the turf-cutters with their winged slane-spades never cut a bank right out. Three steps were carefully left at the end so that the fairies could get up and down the steep brown walls. Besides, nobody was anxious to incur the wrath of St. Colmcille who once got a ducking in a boghole and therefore ordered three steps for every bank. But after the slanesmen had gone home and the spring sun had partly dried the spread turves, women and children came later to foot them and later still to clamp and castle the precious fuel. And had not Aggie been Queen-of the-Bog in her day, sending her brother into town with a surplus twenty loads or more of turf before even the corn was cut? How often now the old woman recalled the sport of the bog, how hot it had been working in the sun, how the children's laughter rang and how the fires crackled among the heather when they boiled old black kettles for the tea, and how the men had cursed when their rhythmic cutting was broken as spades slipped on the old wife's tow, the still-fibrous reeds of lost centuries. Aggie remembered the old days in the bog with a thankful prayer on her lips, for from the hours of sweat and cartloads of turf had come the contents of the tea-caddy, the Jubilee tin that rested so snugly and heavily under the home stack. At seventy, Aggie regarded old age as a calamity to be encountered in the future still remote.

It was not always the need to cut heather for a besom that sent Aggie out to thread her way among the sally bushes, causing redpolls and pipits to rise at the unaccustomed disturbance. She liked to feel she could still care for the communal rights of the neighbours who lived miles away, and the cottagers who one day might return to plant their cut-over plots. But Aggie knew the ways of the bog too well. Next May moon might wane, yet nobody but herself would come out to cut the few odd bits of bank. The great buried forests were laid bare and ravished. Nothing more than a pair of fine gateposts by the orchard remained of the resurrected oaks. Though wanton wildlife ran amok over the melancholy bog, Aggie felt no desolation as she went into the wilderness to pick a bunch of bog-cotton for luck. All of it, even the treacherous, usurping sallies, was part of her kingdom and she reigned over it with a fierce, possessive love. Her memory and imagination together populated the green and brown wastes with so many people that sometimes Aggie was surprised she remembered them. Many was the old song that came floating in her head, many the joke, the flashing eye, and the face of young men she once thought she loved.

Conscious of territorial rights and obligations though she was, Aggie never suffered from avarice. Indeed, as some of her nearest neighbours observed, it was a wonder that she had a penny to her name for none was so generous or open-hearted. Every cub that came with a goat got a luck-penny for himself and a fine feed of boxty. Every housewife who came looking for a setting of eggs was pressed with a taste of Aggie's celebrated elderberry wine, and they never left without fruit or vegetables to take with their eggs. Aggie believed that to dismiss a visitor without a gift was to court ill luck. And this notion applied not only to the humble folk who lived at her own level but also the quality. The rector could easily be satisfied with a section of honey or even a lock of apples. The Master, on the other hand, required different treatment. He only came up the bog pass twice a year, and only that to go shooting. He came to the half-door and gave Aggie a pound note in recognition of the shooting rights on her few acres. Nobody was more courteous to Aggie than the Master, and he extended this even to the point of introducing any of the other quality who might be with him. This was honour indeed as Aggie was the first to own. But she also regarded it as her due, for after all, was it not her own brother who had brought back for the young Master his father's Bible from the war, together with his dying message? Such elevated visitors to Aggie's cottage had to have some remembrance, be it only a rose or sprig of lucky heather, for their buttonhole. The Master was not above taking a glass of buttermilk either, if he had the thirst.

In view of such grand visitors, it was not then surprising that the housekeeper from the mansion house also came to pay her a visit once in a while. Nor was it surprising that Aggie was quite upset when this worthy died, although she left Aggie a fine sewing machine. Aggie was proud of her acquisition but it became a monumental rather than a practical addition to the cottage's effects for Aggie did but little tailoring. What indeed could be done to a sack-apron, which was only changed should she happen to catch sight of the rector or other quality coming up the lane? Hers was a hard life involved almost exclusively with looking after the goats, winning the hay and planting her potatoes. Little time remained to think of big dresses and fancy shoes. Nevertheless, despite her busy days, Aggie did look forward to a visitor coming in for a *ceili* and not just to look for the billy or search for woodcock. When the housekeeper died, Aggie's social life suffered a loss and she, in common with everybody round the whole barony, set to speculating who would be appointed next. Aggie in particular set great store by this for it was by no means certain that the newcomer would find Aggie's company congenial. Weeks went by without the gap being filled. There was just no one to be found in all the neighbourhood capable of filling the post and of bearing at her waist the jingling keys of the mansion house treasures.

Then, one morning, Aggie saw the old gamekeeper lumbering up the path, and she guessed that something had happened at last. The old man set his gun down by the half-door. Speech was no speciality of his so in preparation for what he had to say, he removed the stump of pipe from between nicotined teeth and with the back of his hand wiped his moustache which was exactly like two Shredded Wheats in a breakfast plate. His reluctance to use words was increased on this occasion since he was desperately shy of Aggie. This was because on the day when he had brought the sewing machine, her keen eye had spied a hole in his knickerbockers, which she promptly offered to mend, knowing him to be a widower. People being what they are and matrimonial matters being what they are, the old man had interpreted Aggie's offer as a sign that she was more interested in his widowed state than the hole in his knickers. Aggie had no such thought in her head. Having survived so long alone she was quite decided that no man was going to share her life. The gamekeeper, however, could not be expected to know this and was therefore ready to shield himself against any shaft Cupid might let fly, for he too was content, and quite woman-proof down in the gatelodge.

The gamekeeper's news was brief and to the point. A new housekeeper had come to the mansion house. Aggie was pleased at this, but less so on learning that it was no other than the Master's cousin, a Miss Katie, who was obviously a lady-housekeeper and consequently on a level with the quality herself. This Miss Katie had apparently been to foreign parts and, according to the gamekeeper who had already conversed with her, spoke exactly like all other quality. Sadly, Aggie reflected on this unforeseen situation. She doubted whether she would ever have a visit from so great a personage.

A glimpse of Miss Katie was certain to be obtained when Aggie made her annual pilgrimage to the parish church for harvest thanksgiving which, by good fortune, was the next Sunday but one. With delicate, penguin-like steps, the lady-housekeeper came slowly up the aisle towards the mansion house pew. Without turning her head too much so that her staring was obvious, Aggie could see she suffered from bad feet. And halfway through the sermon Miss Katie coughed with a really fearsome bark. Reports circulating that the lady had only left the fogs of London for her health's sake, seemed now to have substance. Putting out of her mind the rector's harangue which reminded his congregation that it was the Lord who replenished the earth, Aggie thought how much good one of her own renowned herbal cures would do Miss Katie. But to establish contact with her would prove to be an insuperable difficulty, despite the former Master himself having been a patron. In the old days he was a regular visitor, and Aggie's stinking-roger had been such relief to his poor piles. And not only the old Master had benefited—if it hadn't have been for the powerful charm of her hag-tapers the famous black bull would never have seen the show ground of Belfast. A wee taste of the tapers would kill Miss Katie's cough for good, thought Aggie during the doxology.

Months went by. The pullets started to lay, the goats were running dry. A fine but cold winter came on, etching black twigs on a steel-plate sky, engraving frost patterns on the windowpanes, patterns that stayed from one bitter day to the next. Aggie sat by her fire in the evenings hoping a turf would fall across the hearth foretelling a visitor. Though many a turf did fall with a soft thud and a shower of sparks, nobody came. Crickets sang from a dozen secret holes behind the fire, and across the silent ploughlands came the piercing sound of some rabbit caught in a tinker's snare. And when snows lay over the hills, covering the old bog road like a counterpane, never a footprint dinted Aggie's lane, except the gamekeeper's who called in of a morning. His visits even then were not so much to see Aggie as to know the whereabouts of her billy, for the gamekeeper had a wounded leg from the war and was easily tossed.

Then suddenly it was April again and weren't there the grand warm winds sweeping down from the mountains to dry Aggie's last strand of bog. Before May's moon-waning was over Aggie had her underfooting completed. Indeed, on the very afternoon when she was engaged in making her fairy steps, Aggie looked up and saw visitors approaching on the bog road. Mercy! There wasn't even a hope of running up to the house to change her boots and apron. For from the first instant Aggie had discerned the two figures as the Master and Miss Katie. Feeling trapped and helpless, Aggie hauled herself up the bank and stood to receive them. But consternation changed to curiosity when the visitors announced the reason for their call. Might they borrow the boghole? Aggie did not like to display her surprise, but after all, everyone knew that by the mansion house the Master had water enough for drowning kittens or other beasties. She could not imagine what they wanted with the boghole. Surely the Master was not thinking to make a still for a drop of the hot stuff? But they did not keep Aggie in suspense for long, and to be truthful, Aggie felt both a little relieved and disappointed when they told her. Miss Katie's doctor had ordered her to take treatment in the bog. Her poor, crippled feet were to spend two hours every day in the cool amber water.

This news delighted Aggie, both because poor Miss Katie's feet would be better and because her boghole would be the responsible agent. Aggie wondered now why she had not thought of suggesting the remedy herself. While the Master engaged Aggie in polite conversation, asking whether she had made any finds from past centuries as she cut her turf, Miss Katie demurely slipped off her shoes and stockings. Then she sat on the lowest fairy step like a child and dangled her feet in the water. She was clearly embarrassed by this kind of activity but the lines of determination round her mouth showed that she would carry the doctor's orders out to the letter. Despite Aggie's encouragements and assurances that you wouldn't find anything more beneficial in the whole world, Miss Katie just refused to stand in the water as she feared that the bog would suck her under.

With the fine discernment of others' feelings, which is the hallmark of your true gentleman, the Master sensed that Miss Katie would not relax while he remained to observe the bareness of her feet, which looked like two trout in the brown water. She would get no further than perching on the step. So he excused himself and went away down the old bog road again, without ever once turning round. Some of the adventurous spirit which had driven Miss Katie to see life in foreign parts now returned and she asked Aggie to walk up and down the boghole herself, just to prove how safe it was. Ever obliging, Aggie did so and within a week the lady-housekeeper herself stood on the soft mud bottom, and with Aggie nearby marched up and down, the pair of them looking like Biblical oxen on a threshing floor. By the second week Miss Katie did this entirely on her own, and sloshed to and fro through the delicious mud, her fine silks and satins caught up in her drawers, and a big straw hat of Aggie's placed a little rakishly on her head. She secretly looked forward to her daily walk across the fields to the lazy, carefree hours spent in the sharp but splendid air of the bog. And she was such friends with Aggie by now, that Miss Katie promised to come over to the cottage on Sunday to take tea. Aggie, on her part, had forgotten that she ever doubted whether the new housekeeper would visit her.

Miss Katie announced on the Friday that she would be very pleased to do this, in response to repeated invitations from her new friend. This left Aggie two days to make preparations. Such a cleaning she gave the house that it wore a kind of surprised and injured, yet rosy, look which an urchin has after a scrubbing. The two tea-chests in the corner which were the residence of Aggie's broody hens were covered over with the big willow pattern tablecloth. And all the goats, despite their complaints at deviation from routine, were milked out of doors so that they should not eat the fine greenery and flowers which the old woman arranged round the kitchen. Aggie's sister had once been a parlourmaid so she knew what the quality expected. It went without saying (though Aggie had nobody except the goats to whom she might said it) that Miss Katie would have the cup with the beautiful Gothic lettering announcing that it was a present from Bundoran. And there were enough scones and apple tarts on the frail Belleek plates to set a ploughcub dancing. All the spare milk was made into a fine goat's cheese, and was dressed with fennel and spread between fadge bread, a fine cheese the like of which, Aggie felt sure, Miss Katie had never tasted before.

All this took up a great deal of Aggie's time for, besides getting ready for her guest, she had the usual things to do about the house. In consequence it was very late when she climbed the stairs to her loft bedroom on Saturday night, though earlier than usual when she came down them again on Sunday morning. She tethered the goats well away from the house and started making the final preparations. Unlike many similar cottages in the county, Aggie's was well watered and had a grand wee sheugh up the garden for washing the vessels or getting a quick sup for the calves' broughan. Of course, if prolonged dry weather set in and the wooden butt under the eaves was empty, Aggie had to go over a mile to Hazzard's spa well for her spring water. She never allowed the butt to go completely dry for a huge bullfrog lived in it, a creature that had the finest wee curse call in the Six Counties. But what a grand pot of tea the cold, blue spa water made. It was well worth climbing through hedges and over the flax hill to get a bucketful of the lovely stuff.

Sure enough, Aggie had the enamel pail home and under the dresser long before the appointed hour of Miss Katie's arrival. The table was laid, the bread and butter cut, the fire laden with turves so that its flame would be bright and welcoming. A dozen times Aggie took the oil lamp from its hook on the wall to look at herself in the reflector. She deemed it almost important that the pieces of snaring wire she used as hairpins should not be peeping out. And twice she went up to the loft and got into the stays. They had been bought at a rectory bring-and-buy sale during the war. But their efficiency, doubtful from the first, was now seriously impaired because several generations of mice had liberally fed on the stays. The nibbled holes occurred at strategic places, and so Aggie abandoned the idea, and put the stays back where the mice could easily reach them. Aggie was not unduly distressed as she considered herself dressed to kill in her new frock. She had bought it five years previously for her brother's wake and had only worn it once since, when she went up to lay out Miss Katie's predecessor, a connection with her guest of which Aggie was not unaware. Making quite certain the goats were secure and not likely to spoil the grandeur by bolting home and up on to the table to devour scones and flowers, Aggie set off down the pass to meet her visitor.

A sumptuous afternoon had settled over the countryside, though tempered with a little breeze that shivered in the sallies. Aggie did not hurry. She had only got as far as the hump-backed bridge where the last of their cows had been buried, when she heard voices ahead of her, round the bend. As it seemed unlikely that Miss Katie would be talking to the sallies and birches as she herself did, Aggie concluded that the lady-housekeeper must be accompanied, and in a moment she saw that this was so for there was the young Master in his Sunday finery and him not looking a day over sixty. Aggie's heart thumped when she realised how grand her tea-party would be. Not since her brother's wake had the young Master actually crossed the half-door, unlike his father, the old Master, who never hesitated to dash into the cottage for a slice of fadge if he felt hungry while out shooting. Smiles wreathed Miss Katie's face and as Aggie led them up to the house her mind was hardly on their remarks for she was trying to remember the whereabouts of the moustache-cup with the view of Portrush on it. And hadn't the good Lord foreseen the greatness of the day and made her Aylesbury duck lay a large egg that very morning. No man's tea, in Aggie's view, could possibly be considered complete without a duck egg. Miss Katie would be catered for by two of those deep coloured eggs from the Rhode Island Reds.

By the time they reached the house Aggie remembered in what cupboard the moustache-cup was kept and so felt easier and able to play her part in the dialogue of genteel remarks. The lady-housekeeper expressed her delight at the cottage and its cosy rooms, commenting especially on the floral arrangements and the tradesmen's calendars which bore witness to the arrangement of days over a score of past years, and whose pictures lent art to the cottage. She said what a pleasure it was to see *inside* the white walls she had seen so often from the *outside* as she paddled in the boghole. And like great ladies always do when they go cottaging, Miss Katie insisted on seeing everything, even the loft which, as Aggie would have been the first to admit, was hardly a sight for sore eyes. Downstairs once more Miss Katie noticed the big crocks full of fermenting dandelions and asked Aggie about the secret of wine-making. She went further than this on concluding her tour by tasting some elderflower wine, despite it being Sunday. Aggie was a little surprised, but put it down to Miss Katie being English, a condition which Aggie classified with lunacy, both being equal causes of unaccountable behaviour.

Miss Katie gave no indication of discomfort, but as she passed from the kitchen to the other rooms, their cool dankness struck her cheek, telling her how hot the kitchen was. The fire, now roaring away like a blacksmith's, and the strong sun beating on the tiny square of window, combined to make the kitchen into an oven. So with the greatest of tact the lady-housekeeper intimated what a delight it would be to take tea in the garden. The Master concurred, saying what a capital idea that was. Being a woman without prejudices, Aggie soon had a small table outside, and brought out the armchair of coiled straw-rope for the Master. He let himself carefully into it, discovering that, though not uncomfortable, it made him sit in an upright position with his knees near his chin. When she went in to get a milking-stool for Miss Katie to put her dainty feet up, Aggie looked at the Master and thought how much he looked like his uncle, the Colonel, when he had presided at the Petty Sessions.

When Miss Katie settled and was gently fanning herself Aggie went back and forth to the cottage and lilted to herself over the hearth as she wet the tea. And such was the heat and her preoccupation that she could hardly have noticed that Miss Katie was not as relaxed as she appeared to be.

Into a bed of red ashes at the side of the fire Aggie put down the trivet and set her largest teapot on top. Within seconds, two brown eggs and the duck egg were all boiling away together. The eggs made a satisfactory knocking sound against the tin teapot's side, and Aggie did something she had not done for a long time which was to dance four or five steps of a jig to herself. She timed the eggs by experience, knowing that they must be boiled quite hard, for how could you put butter in them to make them tasty if they were soft? As for the tea which was getting steadily darker, the visitors would enjoy a good sup of the black, steaming brew. At last they could all begin. Everything was perfect, and so carried away was Aggie by the bounty of her table that not until she had finished her fourth slice of apple tart did she notice that Miss Katie had eaten hardly anything at all. The lovely brown egg before her was not only half-finished, but rejected and pushed to one side.

A thousand sharp-barbed doubts immediately assailed Aggie. Could it be perhaps that in her foolishness and enthusiasm she had made the tea too black? Without ado she ran into the kitchen for hot water. But as she lifted the singing kettle from its hook she heard Miss Katie and the Master conferring in whispers. Quite unable to fathom what had gone wrong Aggie took the hot water into the garden. Thereafter restraint descended on the entertainment and Aggie felt as if a cloud had been drawn across the bright afternoon sun. A barely polite interval followed and then her guests departed with an abruptness which Aggie could not help but noticing. Aggie walked a little way down the pass with them, despite their protestations that she really need not put herself out, having worked so hard, as she must have, to have produced such an excellent tea. But the table and its scarcely touched food seemed forlorn when Aggie returned to the garden to clear away. She studied the plates, the undiminished pile of scones, and examined the exposed edges of rhubarb pie to detect the presence of flies. True, an unfortunate wasp was trapped in the jam-pot but that was only to be expected in summer. The cups she had brought out for the quality from long hibernation in the cupboards could not have been dirty because she had washed them specially. Admittedly, now that the half-drunk tea had gone cold it did look rather unappetising especially in the way the milk ...

And then, like an Apocalypse, it dawned on her. Of course, the milk. Hadn't the Jehovah's Witness woman left hurriedly for exactly the same reason several years back? Aggie was so ashamed of herself that she dumbly clasped her hands together and wrung them up and down as though she were pumping water. How easy it would have been to have fetched a can of cow's milk while she was over at Hazzard's spa.

Aggie almost hadn't the heart to clear the tea things. She felt like running away, and had there been anywhere to run to she might have done so. As it was, with a heart of lead, she carried in the straw armchair and the milking-stool and put the moustache-cup away in its cupboard again. Every day for a week remorse and depression for such thoughtlessness weighted heavily on her. Aggie, however, being innocent of the world's labyrinthine way of thought and the habit it has of making complex the most straightforward issue, did not imagine that there was more behind the débâcle of the tea-party than just the goat's milk. She had to wait until the gamekeeper's next call to learn that.

He came when a week had elapsed. His slow speech was now a cloak for the discretion with which he divulged the whole truth. Having a sister, and that sister being cook in the mansion house, and the kitchen being the one place where every single item of gossip and scandal could be gleaned, it was not surprising that the gamekeeper not only knew about the tea-party, but knew more about it than Aggie did. The principal interest in connection with his sister's work was that though she was cook, she did not always cook for Miss Katie. The lady-housekeeper's chest apparently, was not the only thing that had been attacked by foul London air. The fogs had descended from lungs to stomach, at least, so the domestic staff at the mansion house maintained. The effect of this was to make the lady-housekeeper extremely fastidious about food. On many days of the week she would take no dinner whatsoever. All that passed her lips were a few pieces of burnt bread such as the city people like to eat and a boiled egg. The toast was cut so thin that the slices were wisps and the egg was so lightly boiled that you could almost pour it out. But most important of all, from Aggie's point of view, was the way the egg was lifted from its saucepan. Miss Katie, who prepared this ghost of a meal herself, used a special wire handle, for she believed that if the water touched human skin, warts would sprout.

At this point in the gamekeeper's narrative Aggie began dimly to perceive the drift of his talk. On the Sunday afternoon, Miss Katie, being exceedingly thirsty, had swallowed two cups of tea before breaking the shells of her brown eggs. When she came to tap the top of one she noticed that a number of tealeaves adhered to the shell, and likewise to the second. This surrealistic juxtaposition of objects not normally related puzzled Miss Katie, and while Aggie's attention was engaged elsewhere, she consulted the Master. Without realising the damage his words were to cause, he answered innocently that in cottages they always boiled eggs and tea together in the teapot. The Master no doubt thought the quaintness of this would amuse his cousin. It had, of course, precisely the opposite effect. Such was Miss Katie's consternation that she had just drunk two cupfuls of egg-water, that she was scarcely able to speak. What dreadful things must now be happening to her already delicate stomach! She imagined thousands of warts already springing up in her insides like mushrooms in the meadows.

Having discharged what he felt was an obligation to Aggie, the gamekeeper went on his way, leaving her aghast. It was not the least consolation for her to realise that the lady-housekeeper too had suffered a week's mental anguish as a result of the tea-party. Looming as plainly as possible before Aggie now was the certainty that Miss Katie would never again visit her nor paddle in the boghole. Aggie was right, for Miss Katie never did, so the old woman's hopes of a friend in the old housekeeper's place were dashed. Nothing could ever persuade Aggie now against her notion that sure and weren't the English a queer set of creatures.

The Hot-Bed

MRS. WILFOE CLOSED THE BOOK. A feeling of general wellbeing possessed her as she locked it away in the inner drawer of her commodious wardrobe. The Book lived in there altogether with her will, marriage certificate, property deeds, bank book, and other documents. Although Mrs. Wilfoe was not unafraid of burglars, it never occurred to her that any man would dare burst into a lady's bedroom, least of all her own. Not being addicted to the Sunday papers whose pages were filled every week with such doings, she regarded her bedroom as criminals in the Middle Ages regarded cathedral sanctuaries, that is, inviolate. Natural caution, however, caused her to lock both the drawer and the wardrobe. After all the sacrosanct security of her bedroom was all that Mrs. Wilfoe could rely on, now that she no longer used the safe.

Disuse of the safe dated from her husband's death because when revealed, the contents of the heavy iron box had dealt her a double blow. While Mr. Wilfoe was alive she had never presumed to pry into her husband's 'business papers' as she called them. Her few pieces of good jewellery had been kept inside the safe, but whenever she chose to wear them, her husband fetched the jewel-box for her. Mrs. Wilfoe admired his carefulness in providing such protection for their valuables. How well the safe kept their secrets! Never in the fifty years of their wedded happiness did Mrs. Wilfoe ever dream her husband kept things in the safe secret from her also. But this was so, and it became all too apparent after his decease when she slipped the long key into the lock herself for the first time.

Her eyes, so lately swollen with weeping for the man who still lay cold and unburied, hardened when she saw the whiskey flask. That was shock number one. Shock number two came later when she went through his papers and found among them a bundle of letters from a woman in Dublin. Mrs. Wilfoe examined them. Shame, anger and jealousy commingled at each neatly-turned phrase, which promised her husband such physical, extra-marital bliss in an astonishing variety of ways, most of which were utterly unknown to Mrs. Wilfoe. She regarded these letters as the loathsome wiles of a disgusting woman, and as soon as she had closely read every one, she burnt them. Nevertheless, in the middle of a sleepless night she would find her mind wandering over their contents, trying to figure out the exact mechanics. Sharply she would reprimand herself for admitting such filthy thoughts, so filthy indeed that asking God's forgiveness for them was quite out of the question. She would be ashamed to let God know that she was capable of harbouring such ideas. Before even her husband's coffin was borne out of the house, Mrs. Wilfoe also destroyed the whiskey flask, with a hammer, and used a shovel to put the pieces in the dustbin. She would never pollute her hands by touching anything connected with alcohol.

After these revelations the safe's presence in the house was unbearable, and she had it carried to the cellar—together with a canteen of cutlery. This wedding gift from her brother-in-law served only to remind her of what she considered the source of her husband's downfall. That his brother had led him astray she was quite convinced. Mrs. Wilfoe did not credit her husband with either attractiveness or wickedness enough to have begun it himself. Her brother-in-law was reckless with money, a failing to be expected from a wine-bibber. Because of such leadership along the primrose path, Mrs. Wilfoe excused her husband's lapse though, of course, she could never forgive him, even though he was but lately dead. Quite definitely, when her hammer smashed the whiskey flask, it was symbolic of her determination that no alcohol would ever enter her house again. Mrs. Wilfoe did not count herself among the 'religious' like the exhibitionists who gave their testimonies on the Diamond during fair days. She was not even 'saved', for she allowed men, though not women, to smoke in the house and enjoy the more innocuous radio programmes. And she had specially bought a nasty little terrier to deal with those who came groping for Jesus on dark winter nights, frightening her out of her wits as they slapped Gospel tracts through the letterbox. Nevertheless she held the opinion that drink was the ruin of half Ireland, and had no doubts at all that the Book would have been less valuable today if she had not remained a strong supporter of the Temperance Movement.

With her husband now gone, Mrs. Wilfoe attached sentiment to the Book for it had been started the week before their marriage. Turning back those pages now, Mrs. Wilfoe loved to dwell over the girlish handwriting which had carefully and precisely entered every wedding present, putting down the exact value also. Her handwriting may have changed during the years, she reflected, but not her careful economical nature. Over the years, page after page was filled, the writing growing closer together and more cramped. To Mrs. Wilfoe this was the sign of increasing maturity and wisdom, but to her husband, the only other person ever to open the Book, it had been indicative of increasing parsimony. In fairness he would never have gone as far as to think of his wife as being mean. She never denied him anything and when spending she did so lavishly. Even the best was occasionally not good enough. Yet something in her attitude, the way she never failed to remind him how *much* this or that had cost, took away the pleasure. He always felt that had his wife spent half as much and refrained from mentioning the cost of things altogether his life would have had more joy. After the birth of their son, for instance, when the pangs and pains were over, she presented him with a reckoning of how much the whole thing had cost right from the first days of her pregnancy. To her, they were interesting facts, as important as the baby's weight at birth. But to Mr. Wilfoe, the total figure was a reprimand, as if his wife were reproaching him for involving her in such expense.

Originally intended for insurance purposes, the Book became an obsession. Every single item of household expenditure went into it, furniture and fittings and clothes. And when worn out or discarded, the items carefully deleted by a red line. Yes, Mrs. Wilfoe could claim that life had treated her well, and the Book was witness to this. Late years had deprived her of former vigour, yet none of her zeal for efficiency had deserted her. The scrupulous care taken by the newly married girl over her housekeeping developed into a science. The Book was Mrs. Wilfoe's secret strength in life. But she was known to be a generous contributor to various charities (she took good care that it *was* known). Her friends made their little jokes about her threepenny-bits, yet admired her tenacity of purpose. Every threepenny-bit that came into her hands was put into a bismuth tablet box, and odd Free State coins were similarly dropped into an empty cocoa tin with a slit in its lid. Twice annually, always on the same date each year, Mrs. Wilfoe had a grand counting day and then the coins were dispatched to the bank. The threepenny-bits went to a leper colony in Africa, and the exchanged value of the Free State coins was divided equally between the local temperance society and the Sunday Defence League. Mrs. Wilfoe's friends also knew that Sunday by Sunday she placed a ten shilling note in the free-will offering envelope at the parish church, besides donating cheques for special appeals. She felt that God could not possibly be dissatisfied with the monetary thanks (more than the required tenth) she returned for all the bounties in the Book.

Yet, paradoxically, she felt no obligation to give a tithe for she regarded herself as custodian only, and not the possessor of the articles recorded in the Book. Soon they would be her son's. Her step was slower than it used to be, her sharp eye less quick in its darting. Almost with astonishment Mrs. Wilfoe realised she had considerably less years to live than those already gone and that they had slipped through her fingers into the past. Instinct rather than reason told her that the present is the past, that the future is an illusion, a mirage to lure the old across the barren wastes of the last years. Yet extreme old age held no fear. She would never want. And death, well that was just the closing of a book, and her son was its sequel. Everything the Book held would be his. She loved Maurice, an emotion not the less rich because she thought of him as her inheritor. Indeed Mrs. Wilfoe could think of him in no terms other than as the future guardian of her property, a position which she regarded as a sacred trust. Had she bequeathed the Holy Grail itself, Mrs. Wilfoe could hardly have been more concerned.

But her heart beat alarmingly fast at least once every day when she thought of the qualifying clause in her husband's will. It stated what was to happen if Maurice died without 'issue'. (How she hated the word 'issue'—so like the Roman Catholics who blinked not so much as an eyelid when they mentioned 'fruit of thy womb' when praying to the Virgin.) Perhaps her hatred of the word was linked with her anger and frustration to think that the whole Wilfoe trust would pass to the brother-in-law's family, if Maurice begat no children. The clause seemed cruel to her, cruel and criminal. The fortune would dissipate once her brother-in-law got his hands on it. Not only was he a drunkard himself but he had bred six sons who all drank like fishes. For many years, before her husband's death, Mrs. Wilfoe buried the problem of Maurice in the limbo of her mind, where unpleasant things she did not want to think about lay in darkness. Maurice was still a young man, she would tell herself. But when his father died Maurice was forty. Five more years had passed since then and he was still unmarried, and showed no sign of becoming so. Clearly, something had to be done. Mrs. Wilfoe needed to be quite certain, before she could even think of dying, that everything was not going to the brother-in-law's family. His sons were welcome to the canteen of cutlery which lay tarnishing on top of the safe in the cellar.

Having no interests in her life, Mrs. Wilfoe found it difficult to fill her days now that her legs kept her to the house. To cover this deficiency she lived entirely for Maurice, vicariously enjoying through him the life of a world larger than her own. She even timed her day to run with his. Despite a growing disinclination to rise early, she was always down in the dining-room in time to hear him say grace before breakfast, though she herself never took anything more at that hour than a glass of hot water. At eleven she had a snack to divide up the morning which she usually devoted to dusting the unused reception rooms. This was not a labour of love, but one of necessity, for Mrs. Wilfoe could not bear her daily woman to touch things for fear that the Coalport china or silver inkstands would get broken, and this was not at all unlikely to happen as each of the gloomy rooms was a clutter of vases, clocks, wax fruit and stuffed birds like the Dutch still lifes of Kalf or van Beyeren.

One of Mrs. Wilfoe's unkinder friends once remarked to another that the house was one of the most luxurious morgues she had ever been in. Mrs. Wilfoe eventually got to hear of this and though she cut the woman thereafter, the remark did not affect her. She simply thought it untrue. Her interest now was to keep it in good order for Maurice—and his bride. As her feather duster flicked in the crevices of a hundred and one knick-knacks her thoughts dwelt on the bride. She accepted as inevitable that there must be one. But at the same time she resented it. As far as Mrs. Wilfoe could see, she would have to find a bride for Maurice. This humiliating situation was not unlike the occasions in her childhood when her nurse had put bitter aloes on her thumb to stop her from sucking it. But she had sucked it all the harder until the terrible taste wore off.

Every hour of her day was filled with schemings and

machinations. Meanwhile, unsuitable candidates for the vacant post of bride had to be kept away. What would that secretary of Maurice's be doing now, she wondered, as she polished the brass of a travelling clock. The girl was attractive and friendly and obviously devoted to Maurice and his career. But he could not possibly marry in that direction. The girl did not come out of the top drawer. Had not Mrs. Wilfoe had to teach her how to answer the telephone? She had rung up her son on the girl's first Monday morning, to be greeted with a vulgar 'Hallo'. Mrs. Wilfoe had at least managed to correct this method of address and taught the girl to say, 'Are you there?' In time the secretary learnt to recognise the voice of her employer's mother and used the ridiculous but proper mode of speaking on the telephone for her, though still using 'Hallo' for everyone else. The secretary noticed that Maurice, when she switched his mother through, always said, 'Are you there?' It became quite a joke between the girl and her mechanic boyfriend. His mother rejected any idea of Maurice marrying his secretary, but she always felt that the girl pushed herself forwards. The truth was that Mrs. Wilfoe could not imagine any girl *not* wanting to marry Maurice.

In this unreasonable and unreasoning way she let her thoughts run on about the girl, and she even mentioned her to Maurice, who had never looked at her in that way and could not even have told his mother the colour of the girl's hair. Yet Mrs. Wilfoe persisted. Wasn't she one of the girl kilties who walked to the Twelfth of July meeting like a horde of Jezebels? And didn't she belong to the girls' pipe band that had ousted the once famous temperance society's brass band? Maurice let such tirades as this slide over him, accrediting these attacks on a perfectly harmless girl as symptoms of his mother's advanced years.

Luncheon brought Maurice home to the big house, the garden of dense evergreen and its drooping trees. He came by bicycle and his mother always met him at the gates, so that they could walk up the drive together, Maurice slowing his pace to hers. This was the first moment in the day when Mrs. Wilfoe really felt that she had Maurice to herself. By the front door she took the newspaper from a basket on the handlebars while he wheeled the machine into the garage. Maurice did not like cars, they interested him as little as women. When she had watched Maurice freewheel down the drive at two o'clock, Mrs. Wilfoe went up to rest but was always downstairs again by five, when Maurice telephoned to say at what time he would be home in the evening. This was usually around six o'clock but sometimes a client kept him late, so causing a ripple of annoyance in the calm surface of his mother's life. As she listened to the last sad song of whaap while she waited for her son, Mrs. Wilfoe made bargains with the Lord. If Maurice was wed before Easter, Mrs. Wilfoe promised she would provide the parish church with new cushions and have the old graveyard tidied up. A good strong country girl, breathed Mrs. Wilfoe scarcely moving her lips, who would breed well and have a bit of her own pin-money, dear Lord.

Occasionally Maurice's mother fancied she could hear her little grandson's happy laughter as he played with his toys in the nursery upstairs. The room would have to be redecorated, of course, and the safety bars at the windows renewed. There was never a woman in these fancies, however, just herself, venerable now that she was a grandmother, and Maurice, with the contentment of fatherhood on him, and the little one who, strangely and beautifully, would resemble the both of them. But the young mother never appeared with the trio. And in spite of so much concentrated thought on the bride problem a shiver still ran through Mrs. Wilfoe when Maurice returned from a trip to London and perhaps told her of a female with whom he had shared part of the journey. For Maurice told his mother everything, or she imagined he had done so ever since the day when he was a little boy and she had caught him in the rhododendrons playing mothers and fathers with his unholy cousins. That Maurice might take after his father in keeping secrets from her and that, metaphorically speaking, he might have a whiskey flask and a bunch of letters never entered her head, and had it done so she certainly would never have considered it as even remotely possible.

Defence of the Book's honour against rape by her in-laws did not become a matter of desperate urgency until Mrs. Wilfoe had her stroke. For a month she was confined to her bed feeling quite unready to cross the bar and meet the pilot face to face, since poor Maurice would be left with no one to look after him. With a strength and willpower which astonished even the family doctor, Mrs. Wilfoe rallied and despite weakness was on her feet again. But she was no sentimental fool and knew that strokes foretell the end. By Easter she was well enough to totter slowly into the garden and cut daffodils for the house. The sun struck her back as she stooped with the scissors. There was promise of summer in the sun, a sign of hope for the future. Mrs. Wilfoe felt a surge of joy at being alive, even though it was only just alive, a joy she had not experienced for many years. She felt as if God in His goodness had allowed her this last chance to see her only child settled and the Book's security assured.

Clasping the daffodils in one hand and her stick in the other Mrs. Wilfoe returned to the house, conscious that a change had taken place inside her during the short time in the garden. She had been given a divine revelation. Possessive was not a word that Mrs. Wilfoe would have recognised as a description of herself. Yet as she entered the furniture-polish-smelling hall she recognised well enough that something very like possessiveness had been lifted, like Pilgrim's burden, from her shoulders. She no longer objected to the idea of another woman about the house, it would be ungrateful to God if she stood in the way of what was clearly His will. During the weeks or months that remained to her, she would fill them with praise to the Lord in that he had vouchsafed to her the opportunity to obtain a bride for Maurice. Not a moment would be wasted. And if God was good and a bride *was* forthcoming, then she would thank Him by putting a new roof on the rectory. Mrs. Wilfoe communicated her intentions to the Almighty in a series of inaudible prayers, uttered while she arranged the daffodils.

Maurice remained in ignorance of the future that his mother and God were working out between them. His interest in girls remained as flaccid as before. He continued to divide out-of-office hours between gardening, his Boy Scout troop and a collection of gramophone records. Although Maurice would have willingly spent more than the one evening a week he already did with his scouts, he felt he should be home to keep his mother company. His father's death had rendered her a most lonely person, and Maurice thought the least he could do was to stay with her as much as possible. Exceptions of course did occur, such as those weekends when he went camping with the scouts, or was over in London. Maurice did not actually sit in the same room as his mother, he considered each of them had a right to a separate existence. As long as his mother could rest happy in the knowledge that he was somewhere about, he considered this sufficient. His gramophone and radio were installed in one of the upstairs rooms. With the volume turned up his mother could hear too, and he imagined that she would think that this formed a bond between them.

Once, with real wickedness in his heart, Maurice reasoned to himself that if he loaded the record player with a few long-playing records, he would be able to slip out of the house. His mother understood nothing of automatic record changing and would think that he was still upstairs. In this way he might have been able to escape for two or three hours. Maurice checked himself as he used the word 'escape'. There was no question of escape. He was always free to come and go as he pleased, and his mother never actually *asked* him to spend his evenings at home. And where would he go anyway? He never drank, and if he stole down to the scouts his mother would be sure to hear of it. Neither could Maurice face the ignominy that would follow if he had an accident in the street. It would easily give his mother another stroke if she discovered such duplicity in him. Having examined the possibility from all angles, the lawyer in Maurice saw quite plainly that such behaviour was both underhand and impractical. He dismissed the matter from his mind, and never thought of it again. The next day he resumed an earlier habit of heavy smoking.

Maurice's forty-sixth birthday fell on a Saturday and he spent it at home. Mrs. Wilfoe had the dining-room table set out with flowers and Maurice's presents as they had always done in the family. Maurice was overwhelmed with the bright, new, blue motor mower. He went over the lawn with it before family prayers. Mrs. Wilfoe watched him through the window, pleased that he liked her gift. But she decided to wait until he came in at eleven o'clock for dandelion coffee before delivering herself of the main issue in her mind. Birthdays had always been a ritual, but since his father's death, added solemnity was given by his mother who invariably hinted that he should begin to think of the future. This morning Mrs. Wilfoe could not afford to miss the opportunity of making her point as plainly as possible. So she had the Book by the coffee things when Maurice came in.

'What's to happen to all this?' she said loudly, waving the Book with one hand, and indicating the room and its still-life composition furniture.

Maurice blushed, as he always did when his mother asked him this question. The succeeding birthdays lined up behind him, seemed to stand accusingly pointing at him. It so looked as if he proposed to do nothing about all this. Yet his mother paralysed him, and he could not have answered even if he would. He was a child again back in the rhododendrons playing mothers and fathers, and feeling terrified by guilt as his mother dragged him away bodily from the evils of the flesh. The bitter scorn she poured on him then had power to lash him still. Unlike previous years, however, his mother did not allow the what's-to-happen-to-all-this to drop so readily. The house seemed filled with the incense of inheritance, its dark corners seemed to anticipate the darkness that would fall should it go to the wine-bibbing cousins. They would not hesitate to bring the whole lot under the auctioneer's hammer.

Maurice kept to the garden for the rest of the day. During the week that followed he stayed late at his office every evening avoiding his mother. But he knew that she was right. With the evidence of the stroke before him he could see she would not rest now until he made some attempt to avoid the awful clause in his father's will. More than anything Maurice did not want to give his mother another stroke. He supposed that if he stirred himself into action he would be able to produce something to keep his mother contented. And having got thus far, Maurice had overcome his greatest obstacle, for when he began seriously to wonder where his eyes might light on a young lady of suitable quality, he found one under his very nose. She had in fact been there all the time, but it had not occurred to him to notice her. But notice her he did on arriving at the scout hut too early one evening. The cubs had not yet gone, and the cub mistress was embroiled in a game of blind-man's-buff. It amused Maurice to see Mavis Withergrow with a cub neckerchief tied round her eyes as she stumbled about. Maurice knew that even at the best of times Mavis had difficulty in seeing through the thick lenses which turned her eyes into peppermint balls.

Maurice sat on a chair at the side of the scout hall looking like a great bear in his shorts, which revealed a length of thick hairy leg disappearing into thick hairy stocking. He studied Mavis. Now that she was blindfolded he could stare at her without embarrassment. That Mavis had been built to a specification for the female of the species there was no doubt. But she did not come in and go out, so to speak, in any of the correct places and though still in her twenties was quite shapeless, when viewed from any angle. No complexion compensated for this serious lack of figure, except a generous sprinkling of acne. Mavis had not much to recommend her, and certainly none of those charms of womanhood on which Maurice very occasionally allowed his mind to dwell. Yet, and this would be difficult to dispute, Mavis was a woman, and it was a woman, practically *any* woman, around which his mother's concern centred. An overwhelming factor in Mavis's favour was that Maurice knew her well, that she possessed a heart of gold despite an appearance so unprepossessing as to be positively homely. As he looked at her now besieged by tiny boys Maurice realised that here was a potential mother, which was all that his father's will demanded. Maurice suppressed his knowledge of Mavis's background, and that she kept the books for her seed-merchant father in the town.

Finding Mavis with her cubs made Maurice think momentarily of his role as a father. He felt quite sure he could do this adequately. Did not the boys sprawl over him as though he was triple-stomached Ts'ai-shen, and did they not demand to see for the twentieth time the bullet wound? They thought him such a hero because he got it in an IRA skirmish while on B-man duty. Having looked upon Mavis in her capacity as a woman, Maurice might well have let matters rest there, in his lethargic fashion. But Mrs. Wilfoe's prayers were not unavailing, for Mavis in her blindfold state walked into the gym apparatus which caused her nose to bleed profusely and alarmingly. Maurice leapt to the rescue with one of the two clean white handkerchiefs he took with him on scout night. There was always some minor injury to be bandaged or limbs tied together for three-legged races, or any of the emergencies which thirty years of scout service had taught Maurice to be prepared for. Mavis, however, could not be dealt with, for after soaking the first handkerchief with blood she then proceeded to do likewise with the second, all without signs of the flood being stanched. Maurice knew there was only one thing to do and he did it—took Mavis to her home, depositing her, bloody and bowed, at the seed-merchant's door.

The novelty of this event appealed to Maurice for he had never in his whole life taken a girl home. That a bleeding nose finally brought such a thing to pass had a piquancy which appealed to that under-developed area of Maurice's brain where his sense of humour was seated. On the following morning, he telephoned the seed-merchant's and spoke to Mavis who, he was relieved to hear, had quite recovered. When he went home to luncheon, Maurice did not tell his mother he had spoken with Mavis, though he had mentioned the bleeding nose to her the previous evening. However, a woman of Mrs. Wilfoe's years and experience of probing into other people's affairs, sensed that Maurice was more animated than usual. As far back as she could remember through each of Maurice's forty-six years he had never, of his own volition, spoken to her of a girl before.

Maurice's taciturnity arose not so much from a desire to hide the matter from his mother as because he could not find very much to say about Mavis. After all , his interest in the girl was primarily for his mother's sake, so he should have been anxious to laud his success so far. But what *could* he say about Mavis? Perhaps he suffered a little feeling of guilt because he had not made much personal effort to find a girl, and that in thinking of Mavis as a bridal candidate he had taken the easy way out. Despite her keenness to get him and the Book in safe hands, Maurice could well imagine the sarcasm his mother would use over Mavis. He heard his mother on numerous occasions making tirades against the cousins. He had no wish to involve the innocent Mavis in such invective. With the skill of a surgeon removing diseased tissue, his mother would no doubt point out how plain and pasty the girl was, how clumsily she walked and how badly she dressed, and how stupid she looked in those great thick spectacles. His mother would fail to be impressed by the fact that one day Mavis would inherit her father's shop which must be worth quite a bit. Mrs. Wilfoe would merely remind him that the shop was one of the town's jokes because a dozen cats or more lived in the shop window amongst the seed potatoes and tulip bulbs. And as for Bloody Willie, well she could not stand the man. Maurice appreciated his mother's dislike of Mavis's father. Mrs. Wilfoe found him objectionable not because, like everyone else, of the dreadfully bloodshot eyes which gave him his nickname, but because she regarded him as a rogue. He had once sold Mrs. Wilfoe some gladioli bulbs which bloomed with a colour quite different from that advertised.

But in making this assessment of the way his mother would react to the impinging of Mavis in their lives, Maurice was quite wrong. Among Mrs. Wilfoe's less pleasant characteristics was her determination, and indeed one of her favourite sayings was the one about Lot's wife looking back. She had made her bargain with God. He had sent a rapid answer to her prayers. It was hardly her place to criticise the girl whom, in His infinite wisdom, God had sent. Mrs. Wilfoe was prepared to sacrifice her own wishes and desires. And so she refrained from leading Maurice a dance, and driving him to exasperation until he finally abandoned the girl, as Maurice always eventually abandoned anything of which his mother disapproved. There was even the possibility that the girl would turn out to be a good breeder—an idea which Mrs. Wilfoe contemplated only within the respectable enclave of her bedroom, the proper place for such thoughts.

So it came about that Mavis, slowly and decently, was drawn into the Wilfoe vortex. Mrs. Wilfoe began to see more and more of Mavis. Acquaintance did not cause Mrs. Wilfoe to disapprove of Mavis any the less, but she was forced to admit that the girl would at least solve all their problems. At least Mavis was not like most modern girls, useless fly-by-nights who could neither cook nor sew, and showed no inclination to learn how to be a good wife and mother as she, God knew, had been. Mavis was useful in the garden and shared Maurice's concern over it. She also kept a pair of knitting needles handy in the house. Mavis was, in fact, never still. As long as any jobs remained to be done she could not sit idle. Neither was she a chatterbox and gossip, but was content to let Mrs. Wilfoe do all the talking, of which she did a great deal, rehearsing for Mavis's benefit her own experience of married life. Mrs. Wilfoe's story always stopped short, of course, at the point where she had opened the safe to find the whiskey flask and bundle of letters.

As best she as she knew how, Mrs. Wilfoe concealed her opinion that Maurice could and should have done better for himself. At the same time, however, she justly recognised that he might have done worse. That baggage at the office, for instance, with the beetroot lips. Suppose Maurice had decided to bring *that* to the house. Mrs. Wilfoe shuddered when she thought how brazen the hussy was. The only thing she really regretted about Mavis was that she came from tradespeople. What induced Maurice to stoop so low and rake about among the lower orders,

Mrs. Wilfoe could not imagine. It was tantamount to Maurice throwing away the benefits of his education, which had given him such a fine cultured voice, and throwing his whole career into jeopardy, for what would Maurice's clients and fellow-lawyers think when they saw Mavis hooked over his arm? Even in the face of what practically amounted to humiliation Mrs. Wilfoe would not give way. She realised that God moved in a mysterious way His wonders to perform. To accept pain and sacrifice, to face them with a light heart, to face the world (she saw almost nobody these days except her daily help, a cousin of hers and Maurice) with a smile, so that it, the world, would approve and say, 'Ah! Mrs. Wilfoe has trouble and sorrow, but see how bravely she bears it!'—this was her path of duty. Actually, of course, the world did nothing of the sort. That infinitesimal part of it which knew of her, regarded her as a selfish old woman. Even the charities to which she sent the threepenny-bits considered that she ought to send more. However, the world was ever vulgar and insensitive, it knew nothing of the Book and Mrs. Wilfoe's bold crusade to save it.

As far as things went, Mrs. Wilfoe accepted Mavis. But life being as complex as it is, certain other approvals had to be gained, notably that of Aunt Martha. She was not Maurice's real aunt at all, but his mother's cousin. A shortage of relatives on the maternal side had necessitated the invention of an aunt for little Maurice, for Mrs. Wilfoe had been quite determined to shield her young son from the evil influence of the cousins on his father's side. And although Maurice's mother was the first to admit that of late years Aunt Martha had become, well, a little peculiar, she nevertheless recognised that Aunt Martha was the right sort of relative to keep in with since her father had been chaplain to the Lord Lieutenant in the good old days when God and Queen were honoured in Dublin. And because Maurice was nicely placed in her will, it was only right to invite Aunt Martha to come and give Mavis a look over.

Arrangements were made accordingly and a weekend fixed for both Mavis and Martha to stay overnight. Mavis cycled out of the town after Saturday closing at the seed-merchants. As the wheels spun beneath leaning elms and two ribbons from a light blue dress streamed behind her, Mavis did not look altogether unattractive. Happiness rather than beauty was responsible for this, as Mavis had become fond of Maurice. She held a sensible straw hat for Sunday on to the handlebars more firmly, and told herself that by marrying Maurice Wilfoe she could have done considerably worse. They held a number of interests in common, scouting and gardening particularly. Indeed, the parcel of young chrysanthemum plants she carried out in her basket were all bedded out and watered by Maurice before supper.

Mrs. Wilfoe had thought she had made it quite plain in her letters to Aunt Martha who and what Mavis was, and what connection the girl had and hoped to have with Maurice. But so peculiar had Martha become that she got it all mixed up and thought Mavis was already a relative. So supper began with a series of strange remarks from Aunt Martha, each of which had to be tactfully corrected by Mrs. Wilfoe. By the time dandelion coffee came in Aunt Martha was fairly in the picture. Not until the two 'children' as Mrs. Wilfoe called them, were out on the lawn preparing Sunday's vegetables, did Aunt Martha catch on to the idea that she had been asked over for the purpose of expressing an opinion about Maurice's future bride. Mrs. Wilfoe naturally did not tell Aunt Martha that whatever she might say, her own mind was made up and that the deed was as good as done, and that as Maurice's mother her concern was to protect Maurice's interest in Martha's will.

Now that the function of her visit was clear to her, Aunt Martha sat near the drawing-room window and fastened her beady eyes on the young pair. It was a hopeful sign that the girl appreciated that Sunday's vegetables should be prepared on Saturday. She must at least realise that only the minimum of domestic work could happen on a Sunday. But Mrs. Wilfoe, who sat beside Aunt Martha and also peeped through the net curtains, was greatly alarmed. She hoped that Aunt Martha had not observed what thick chunks of potatoes Mavis cut off as she peeled them. Disquieting ideas attacked Mrs. Wilfoe—was the girl a waster? Aunt Martha, however, did notice things at supper time. While the other three intimated that they would take cocoa, Mavis said she would like a nice cup of tea like she always had. Such a common little thing, was the mental note made by Aunt Martha. But this was nothing compared with her horror at the housemaid's teacup the girl left afterwards. With an all-out effort, Mrs. Wilfoe tried to distract Aunt Martha's attention from this new calamity. How _could_ Mavis be so common as to drain her tealeaves up the side of the cup?

Mrs. Wilfoe clenched her hands in determination. She was not going to let details obscure main issues, however shocking the details might be. It was not likely that Mavis would indulge in tea-cup fortune telling, but was the girl, and this was truly a dreadful idea, was she fortune hunting? The Devil tempted Mrs. Wilfoe with many such evil notions, but she stood steadfastly by the girl God had sent. All the same, as she went slowly up to bed that Saturday night serious doubts about Mavis's suitability dogged her footsteps.

The Lord's Day dispelled Mrs. Wilfoe's fears with its warm sunshine and stillness. The day passed successfully enough, divided between devotional reading and divine service in the morning and evening. Maurice and Mavis went for a short walk in the afternoon and Mrs. Wilfoe tactfully suggested that she and Aunt Martha had tea before their return. The children would have theirs in the garden so that Mavis' table manners might escape scrutiny. Meanwhile, she had not been idle. The formality of Aunt Martha's approval was almost a foregone conclusion now that Sunday was all but over, and Mrs. Wilfoe was confident of some announcement of engagement. Planning with that foresight of which the Book was such excellent evidence, she was already thinking in terms of a honeymoon. She wanted the problem of the heir well on the way to solution before God, in his own good time, should take her. To this end she spent Sunday afternoon scanning the advertisement columns in the back numbers of her _Sunday Defence_ magazine looking for a suitable teetotal hotel. Well before teatime her efforts were rewarded with such an establishment on the coast of County Down. There was no need to let the others know of her research, for Mrs. Wilfoe was hoping Aunt Martha might be generous and put her cottage at Donaghadee at the newly-weds' disposal. The saving on this would be most gratifying. She could hardly wait now for Sunday to end, so that Maurice might put the vital question to Mavis before her return to the town next day.

By the time Mrs. Wilfoe had coiled her white plaits into a pilgrim bun at the back of her head on Monday morning, the great decision had been made. Her grooming was a hurried affair because Mavis was due in town for the opening of the shop. From her window she saw Maurice going into the garden with Mavis. All was going to plan, except that he was directing her into the rhododendrons. Mrs. Wilfoe had never fully recovered from the day she found the little boy playing mothers and fathers there. It was most tactless of Maurice not to remember that incident, for it struck her as indecent of him and Mavis to be screened by the bushes. Mrs. Wilfoe's house-shoes seemed obstinate and refused to go on easily just because she was in a hurry. She had to get down to the hall and be the first to congratulate Mavis. Would she have to kiss the girl, she wondered?

But she need not have worried.

Hoping for a glimpse of the young pair she looked from her window. Maurice was striding up the drive with a face as black as thunder and, under the elms lining the road, Mrs. Wilfoe caught sight of a figure flying along. It was Mavis, pedalling as hard as she could go.

Faster than she had moved for years, Mrs. Wilfoe was downstairs. The affair was off. There would be no wedding, no engagement. Maurice's mother had never seen him so cross, and she was even a little afraid of the fierce look in his eye. The words of chiding which rushed to her lips and away again, a torrent of criticism at his bungling, was stemmed when she heard how the girl had received Maurice's offer of marriage. Mavis was expecting it, but had been none the less delighted and flattered—but it had to be on her own conditions. Maurice was almost inarticulate with her preposterous demands. He, Maurice Wilfoe, with all the promise before him of being the next coroner was expected to go and live with the seed-merchant. Mavis expected him to place his cycle against the window full of cats, and climb up the stone steps that were cluttered with hoes and bags of bone-manure, to eat his meals with Bloody Willie who never took his bowler hat or leather leggings off summer or winter. Maurice had never been so mortified. The suggestion was outrageous as was Mavis's whole scheme for the future. She could not possibly leave her father with no one to look after him, and so she thought that Aunt Martha could live with Mrs. Wilfoe.

This piece of impertinence rendered Mrs. Wilfoe impotent of speech or action. Her hand shook so much that she could not hold her breakfast glass of hot water. Maurice rushed out to his office in a rage, slamming the front door—a thing he had not done before in all his forty-six years. He had regained sufficient consciousness of his surroundings by the time he had arrived to snap Beetroot Betty's head off when she inquired, as usual on a Monday morning, if he had enjoyed his weekend. An hour later the telephone rang and Beetroot Lips told him that his mother wished to speak to him. Speech had returned to Mrs. Wilfoe when Aunt Martha came downstairs. Mrs. Wilfoe told her the morning's events, evoking from Martha expressions of horror but solicitation that they were well rid of such a wilful-minded waster. But on going upstairs into Mavis' but lately vacated bedroom another shock awaited them. Housemaid's teacups were nothing compared with what they found.

There was no denying the evidence. Mavis was a hot-bedder. Not only did the room stink of godless strumpet's musk, as Mrs. Wilfoe called perfume, a state enhanced by the tightly closed window, but the bed was made. Even the counterpane was over it, the counterpane that Mrs. Wilfoe's own mother had taken three whole winters to make. The two ladies could hardly believe their eyes. That girl had got straight out of her bed and made it again immediately, without airing it. As though expecting to find signs of immorality under the bedclothes, Mrs. Wilfoe ripped them back and draped them over the iron rail to air, and saw at once that the mattress had not been turned. Aunt Martha flung the window open. Mrs. Wilfoe confided that no one in *her* house had ever made a hot-bed before, and, for her part, she was exceedingly glad that the girl would not be coming back to continue such vile, unhealthy practices. She hardly dared to think what horrors the living-rooms above the seed-merchant's must contain.

Later, while emptying the wastepaper basket, Mrs. Wilfoe's daily help had sense enough to examine a paper bag which Mavis had screwed up and thrown away. Inside she found quite a number of cigarette butts. It was now plain that without doubt Mavis would have sent the Book's whole contents up in smoke, literally. And this was to say nothing of drink, for a mysterious cork was also found, clear indication that Mavis was a secret wine-bibber as well as a waster, smoker, and hot-bedder. Looking back Mrs. Wilfoe could see now that nothing better could have been expected of Mavis. The girl had never belonged to the Band of Hope and her father, Bloody Willie, had constantly and consistently refused to display Temperance Society literature in his shop windows.

Partly to console Mrs. Wilfoe, but more to catch any last titbits of scandal, Aunt Martha said she would delay her departure until after mid-morning coffee. So she was in the house when Maurice telephoned again later, and she hovered about the hall hoping the hear snatches of the conversation. But Mrs. Wilfoe merely said 'yes' and 'no', so Martha had to wait until the old-fashioned receiver was replaced on its hook and then covered with its tea-cosy. In a rather excited voice from which all traces of former vexation were absent, Maurice told his mother of his plans for the next week. The new young assistant scoutmaster wanted him to go over to England for the big jamboree. Maurice appeared to have forgotten Mavis already. Mrs. Wilfoe heaved a sigh of relief. On finding the hot-bed she had had a vision of the Book and all it stood for going to pieces in the hands of that waster. Now perhaps Maurice would find a nice respectable girl over in good Christian England.

After Aunt Martha had gone, Mrs. Wilfoe went to her bedroom, got out the Book and, clasping it to her breast, thanked God for deliverance from evil. But He would have to move pretty smartly, she thought, if He was to get Maurice a bride during the course of the next week.

Man in a Pub

HAVE THIS ONE ON ME ... AND don't talk to me about pantomime. Even if it's in the Midlands, it's something to look forward to. If you've been resting all autumn, the idea of at least nine weeks' regular pay is, to put it mildly, attractive. 'Even if' are words to be used about the Midlands. At Brighton or Bournemouth, say, pantomime is different. No sooner are you out of the stage-door than a salty gale seizes you by the lapels and batters you all the way along the front to your digs in North Street. Sometimes, surprisingly, you can bake in the sunshine or be really bold and go for a swim with the old men like we did one year at Torquay. Not so the Midlands. The sky is grey. It rains. Or perhaps it snows feebly. Then it rains again. And the sky is grey. There are the pubs, of course, where you can go. They are full of down-to-earth people. The bars are scrubbed and Victorian so that you can make remarks about solid teak counters and cut glass and weren't things marvellous then. But everybody really hates it. As soon as the nine weeks of pantomime are done, none of the theatricals would dream of staying in the earthy Midlands, not even to see the sooty sort of spring which makes the arboretums sadder than ever.

I know what I'm talking about. There's nothing you can tell *me* about panto in the Midlands. There's always a first time, naturally. With me it was *Cinders*. A grimy train took me to the station. When I found the theatre (Alhambra! You never saw anything *less* Spanish or Moorish or whatever it is, in your life) the stage-doorman recommended digs. The *Fox and Grapes*, he said, was about the best I'd find round there, seeing as it was clean but at the same time a place to get a drink like after the show. The pubs, you see, he said, close at ten.

The *Fox and Grapes* was in a long straight street. And if you have already guessed that the gasworks was at one end and a brewery at the other, you're right. Bag in hand I rang the bell and the door was opened by a big woman, aged about fifty but who could claim forty-two without making herself look silly.

'So you're the Baroness!'

Well, people have called me some things, in my time. 'No.' I drew back from the pudgy hand with lots of rings on it that she held out. 'Only the stage manager,' I said, trying to sound important in a modest way.

'Oh,' she said, disappointed, 'are you. Well I've been expecting you, Alfie on the door gave me a tinkle. I'm sorry, though, you'll have to put up with the back double. Jack Frost's there too. Hope you don't mind—comfy beds.'

I was discovering fast that in panto in the Midlands, there was no point, absolutely none, in minding about things. I left my bag, refused a cup of tea and hurried back to the theatre. The front curtain was up. Two women were cleaning along the rows of seats in a defeated sort of way. One or two bleak lights showed up the usual backstage squalor. By some half-finished flats an elderly woman in baggy tweeds was arguing in a loud voice with the stage carpenter. She was winning. It just had to be Mrs. Willoughby Jorden-Soames of *The Four Black Beauties*. Her animals were the ones which were going to pull Cinderella's coach. We hoped. I didn't escape in time. Instinct had warned her that I was stage manager.

'My friend, my friend,' she cried, clutching my arm. 'Tell this man they must do it.'

The local staff, apparently, expected her 'children' to walk up the five steps to the entrance door. Whereas she expected the entire work of scenery building to stop while a ramp was constructed for the ponies. She pressed me to keep an eye on the 'children'. Having been a matelot, the stage carpenter could adequately express his feelings. But he had the sense to wait until Mrs. W.J.-S. was out of hearing. His language shocked even me. But he made the ramp nevertheless.

Well, that was the start of things. There was only a week to go before the show opened on Christmas Eve. None of us believed it would except the producer. He had stomach ulcers and was ignored by everybody. Later that afternoon the babes from the local dancing academy were on stage to rehearse a skipping number. But I didn't have much time for them as the next row had broken out, between Jack Frost and the dress designer. I could do nothing, for neither would let me get a word in and screamed at each other, both together, at the tops of their voices.

The outcome was that Jack Frost swept out of the theatre saying that *he* wasn't going to be dictated to by any bitch, and let *them* try to sparkle twice nightly by applying silver paint and that anyhow, if they thought he was going to get himself up in *that* old thing (referring to the dress designer's Jack Frost costume) then they had another think coming because, though the designer might not know it, Vesta Tilley had been dead for donkey's years and *he*, Jack Frost, had no wish to look like the old cow trying to make a come-back. In short, he would make his own blasted costume and they could all go to hell—'including you' he said venomously to me on the way out.

Half an hour afterwards he was back again with yards and yards of some material which looked like, but which could not possibly have been, silver lamé. He also had thousands of sequins. There and then he started to make his own costume. His temper had subsided and he was sweetness itself. 'I'm sorry,' he said between snips of the dress designer's shears, 'if I was rude just now. But *really*, people are the end.' Sequins were Jack Frost's great fancy. During any show for the next nine weeks I was to find him between his dances, sewing on sequins. He shed them as fast as he could fix them. But on good days, like matinées, he would have time enough to sew on two or three hundred.

Luckily, despite the landlady's threat about the back double, I never did have to share with Jack Frost. A rather fruity Father Time turned up later in the day. For a reason I could never discover but only suspect, Jack Frost fled from the *Fox and Grapes* and took up temporary residence nearer the theatre with a little friend he met in the town. When I went for supper at the digs the Baroness had arrived.

Actually, the Baroness was our top billing and had twice the packet of local Cinders. There was no side with him, though. He preferred to share a room at the *Fox and Grapes* rather than lord it at the *Grand*. He was, as our landlady put it, a very human man. I only had him for four out of seven nights because at weekends his wife and family came in their caravan, so that the Baroness was on the car park leaving room for me.

The Baroness's was the only costume which had been made in London. This caused a great shindy too, so that the curtain really almost never went up—as I overheard our landlady telling her daughter over the phone. 'That Baroness,' she said, 'came in here and went straight and packed his cases. If it wasn't for me, Ivy' (Ivy was the daughter—the one whose wedding photo stared at us breakfast, dinner, high tea and supper for nine weeks) 'there wouldn't be no pantomime.'

This I knew was literally true. After the season's biggest row the Baroness had cleared out and we all said that was the end of *him*. Mrs. Willoughby Jorden-Soames, with whom the Baroness had fought, also left the theatre and we all said that was the end of *her* too. Apparently, though, our landlady heard movements upstairs and, as she knew we were all at rehearsal, thought it was a burgular, as she called them. Anyway, she calmed the Baroness down with cups of tea and a bottle of rum from under the stairs. He told her all about it. Then, when he was fairly high, she packed him off back to the theatre and phoned me. 'The Baroness is all right now,' she said, 'but you'd better settle that woman yourself.' 'That woman' was Mrs. W.J.-S. I went off myself to cope with her and brought her back, making cross-my-heart promises that such a thing would never happen again. She kept saying she should think not indeed. For the rest of our run she and the Baroness did not exchange one single word.

It all happened because of the Baroness' dress and the stage lift. The Alhambra was built on a hill and to get up to the stage from street level everything had to go up in this lift. Things were well under way for the dress rehearsal. The boss was down from London twiddling the script in his hand, worried to death because he knew, as we all did, what great difficulty the poor Baroness would have in keeping to the Lord Chamberlain's censored version. With any lewd backchat from the gallery he would give better than he got.

The producer was here, there, and everywhere, pretending in front of His Nibs that he was on top of the show, though a first year Tiller could see that he was itching to be off in his Jaguar to his other panto in the Potteries. The electricians were perched up in the flies, the conductor was perched on the rostrum. Then from the lift-shaft came the most terrible din in which the cries of *The Four Black Beauties* were mixed with the Baroness' curses.

The lift, of course, had to carry up both ponies and principals. The Baroness had that north-country manner of getting on well with people and with animals too. Two cats and a budgerigar lived in his caravan. To establish good relations with the ponies he had laid in a stock of lump sugar. It was just bad luck that he forgot to bring any for the dress rehearsal. He was nervous enough though, and so were the ponies, for going up in the lift one of them made a terrible mess over the Baroness's grand London dress.

Vexed beyond endurance the Baroness gave the pony a slap on its rump. But so well bred were the four little Shetlands that they took exception to this and tore the wonderful dress almost to shreds. The Baroness and Mrs. W.J.-S. set to immediately and practically came to blows. He stormed out and went, as I have explained, back to the *Fox and Grapes* to pack up and leave. She also stormed out and later went back to the ponies' stable, where I found her later. She refused to let the animals go on stage. The dancing babes had to pull Cinders' coach for the dress rehearsal and would be doing so, we thought for the remainder of the show—*if* it went on.

Next morning, Christmas Eve, with the contracts being waved in everyone's faces, a truce was drawn. Mrs. W.J.-S. agreed to the ponies' appearance on the strict understanding that only I, and nobody but I, should conduct the ponies up in the lift. The Baroness was sufficiently mollified by the arrival on the night train of a new and if anything, a more resplendent dress than the ruined one. *Cinderella* opened at two-thirty on Christmas Eve to a packed, expectant, appreciative but totally unsuspecting house.

Before we knew it, the first week was over, with no hitches. Everyone began to relax a bit and Jack Frost was seen, twice, talking to the dress designer. I saw little of the *Fox and Grapes* but it was pleasant enough. Three principals from the panto were staying there as well as the business manager, an old-timer who found managing more profitable than performing. He was well in with His Nibs but none of the cast curried his favours for they distrusted him. In any case, the others worked for the same company as he did outside pantomime, and felt jealous of the manager because His Nibs gave him a month off every autumn specially for the old boy to go and pick his walnuts.

He never bothered me and I got used to seeing him wandering about the *Fox and Grapes* in an old pair of nylon pyjamas which had been given him, he said, by Gertrude Lawrence in New York. Some of the others commented that the pyjamas looked as if they *were* Gertrude Lawrence's. You know what the theatre is for gossip. But although the business manager did not go down well, most people had to admit that he was necessary. Otherwise Jack Frost would have had half-a-hundred-weight of sequins down on expenses and Mrs. W.J.-S. would have fitted out her ponies with new rainproofs and galoshes for going to and from the theatre.

As the show went on and the routine settled, it soon became apparent that nothing was going to wear us down so much as Mrs. W.J.-S. and her animals. The five of them together took up more backstage time, trouble, effort and nervous energy than the rest of us added together. Even Jack Frost did not use as many shampoos as went on the manes and tails of those wretched creatures, which is saying something. The audience wallowed in it—the act I mean, not the shampoo. After a matter of only minutes Cinderella got herself dragged off in her coach and that was that. But from morning till night we heard of nothing but ponies. The business manager went red in the face every time the outrageous fodder bills came in from the old railway stables.

Really, of course, we were all waiting for it to happen. We had no idea *what* but something would, because Mrs. W.J.-S. was the sort of woman to whom things always happened. Luckily for the show, the crisis happened at the end of a matinée. Unfaithful in my promise to Mrs. W.J.-S. to take the 'children' up and down in the lift myself, I had trained the call-boy to do it, the little Shetlands knew perfectly well where they were going. And the ride in the lift was good for a few lumps of sugar each. Nobody had given a single thought to what would happen if the lift stuck with the animals in it as, being antiquated, it was likely to do, and on that afternoon did so. I arrived just in time to see Mrs. W.J.-S. on her knees calling down the lift-shaft.

'All right, Tinker darling, Mother's here.'

Cinderella, also in the lift with all her coach finery, was clearly heard to say *merde*—a word she had picked up in a French night club where she once worked.

Mother, though, wouldn't wait until we could get our electrician on the job. Oh no, she went and phoned the brigade. Thinking the Alhambra was going up in smoke they rushed two engines straightaway and the theatre suddenly filled with eager firemen. The eagerness wilted when they saw that there was in fact no fire. But the sight of so many uniforms and sound of so many feet and voices put panic into the ponies who, until then, couldn't have cared less about being stuck in the lift. So they lashed out with hooves and everything, wounding poor Cinders. Neither she nor the ponies were in a fit state to go on in the evening, despite the bevy of doctors and vets which was rushed in.

Secretly, though, we all loved Mrs. W.J.-S.; for, like most of her type, all the bluster and fuss covered a good-natured, easily-hurt soul. And though she apparently lived for nothing but her four 'children', we all knew in fact that her bedridden husband came before all else. They owned some kind of horsey place in Devon where she did all the training and breeding—even teaching the 'children' to bend their knees for curtain calls. Every time she arrived at the theatre with the animals she flew to the phone to tell her husband that they had once again got safely there. After the show she rang him again to report on the 'children's' performance. Poor Tinker had a bad habit of disgracing himself on the stage. She could be strict, and any of them who gave a bad curtain call weren't allowed to hear 'Father's' voice saying goodnight over the phone.

Typically, I didn't find out what the others thought of her until the panto's last night. The Baroness was going to throw a party. Nobody could think of a better place to have it than the *Fox and Grapes*. Fortunately the air was clear again after a fearful *crise de nerfs* between the landlady and the business manager. She came in from the pub one evening at her usual hour. I was alone in the sitting-room.

'Are you Catholic?' she demanded suddenly. Without waiting for an answer she went on, 'I've told him. It's disgraceful. I've never seen the like, not in all the years in this house, nor when we was living in Barrow. I told him I said ... '

She railed against the manager for ten minutes, bringing in Ivy ('That's my married one, you know'—who could *not* know in that house?) and her dead husband as evidence that they hadn't never seen anything like it. What *it* was, I couldn't gather for a long time. I searched for a reason that could upset a Catholic— could it be something to do with her delicious steak and kidney

pie being eaten on a Friday? But no, it wasn't. Eventually she ran
dry of insults and said, 'I'll just run up to his room and get it.'

I could not think of anything terrible which the business
manager could have done. The landlady reappeared in the
sitting-room holding up a beautiful embroidered waistcoat
which I had seen the manager wear. It matched Gertrude
Lawrence's pyjamas excellently.

'Well', I said still in innocence, 'what about it?'

As though she dared hardly touch it the landlady laid it over
the armchair.

'That was a *priest's*,' she said weightily. For a moment her
meaning eluded me. It seemed most unlikely that a priest would
sport a waistcoat like that. Then the awful truth dawned. The
waistcoat was once a chasuble. The landlady repeated to me
what, with more vehemence, she said to the business manager.

'It might be twenty years since I was in church, but I've never
seen such disrespect.'

But she was a cunning one, our landlady. Machiavelli
couldn't touch her. Anyway, she made the business manager
give up his waistcoat. The poor thing had little enough hair left
and he held on to his few wisps like grim death, or rather, his
herbal treatments held them on. One night, in the middle of
supper, as sweet as a May morning, she says to him, would he
mind not brushing his hair in the bathroom as all the falling-out
hairs were blocking up the sink. Though, she added, she for one
was not surprised at him going starko on top, seeing as how he
had the curse of a priest on him. After that, we never saw the
waistcoat again. Jack Frost swore that the manager was going to
the church down the road for the old candle game.

That affair was, thank heavens, a thing of the past by the time
the Baroness announced his last performance party. We were in
fact all in the right mood. The panto was behind us with all its
petty grievances which looked large at the time. About midnight
Jack Frost piped up 'She's missing.' And so she was. Mrs. W.J.-S.
Then we all remembered that she was not being stand-offish but
couldn't join our party because of the 'children'. She would

never allow anyone else to take the 'children' back to the stables when the show was over. The ponies were well used to drinking. As a nightcap 'Mother' always gave them a bottle of stout with their bran. But parties, she considered, were bad for them. In fact she was a hypochondriac over the 'children'. They were rarely out of her sight, not even at night for she slept in their stable.

The suggestion came from none of us in particular. We just moved out of the *Fox and Grapes* as a very noisy party and made our way downtown. Jack Frost had been elephant-boy in a circus once, years before. He knew the way to the Midland Railway stables where 'mother' and 'children' lived. On the way I noticed that nearly everyone carried a bottle. I realised then the estimation in which Mrs. W.J.-S. was held. Grand and county though she was, to the panto people she was an old, experienced pro. They would never have dreamed of missing her out of the last night party. Or the animals either, though Jack Frost was fonder of them than any of us. He took them the *Fox and Grapes*' last bottle of port. They had it in a corn-mix and the poor things got quite tiddly, as they had already had their stout.

Behind the railway station Jack led us into a yard and up a long ramped gallery which gave on to tiered stables. 'The horses which pulled railway carts used to kip in these, poor things. You can still smell them,' he informed us. On one of the doors was a panto poster, so we knew that the family of five must be inside. The stable was like a prison scene during the French Revolution and Mrs. W.J.-S. looked exactly as if a tumbril was about to collect her. Tears had streaked her face and she was far from the party mood. But instead of fussing, somebody got a couple of large gins down her. She cried again, dried her eyes on Jack Frost's handkerchief and blew her nose on the Baroness'—the reconciliation of the dress rehearsal row. Then she told us the story since the last curtain came down and she had brought the 'children' home.

I was prepared for the worst. Her old man had died I guessed. There must have been a last phone call to the theatre, and then nothing. But the tears were much more serious. That very evening, while we were making pigs of ourselves at the *Fox and Grapes*, a Ministry of Agriculture man called at the stables to check up on the livestock. Foot-and-mouth disease had come to town. No animals could be moved in or out of the town. Two more gins had to be administered at this point. Mrs. W.J.-S. could not bear to think of her 'children' spending one night more in those stables. And I could quite see why. The stables were damp, airless, and full of rats. The fact that Mrs. W.J.-S. had lived herself in those conditions for nine weeks struck us with chill feelings. Her loyalty to the 'children' was nothing short of heroic.

'But you mustn't stay here another minute,' said Cinderella. She had forgotten her feud with Mrs. W.J.-S. over the lift incident and the claim for damages.

'Oh, it's not me,' replied the ponies' 'mother', 'it's Tinker.'

Tinker was always the trouble. It was he had first panicked in the lift. It was he who misbehaved on the stage and threw temperaments. Now he was sickening. He was too highly bred to stand up to the strains and excitement of the past weeks. And his chest had developed a nasty cough from the damp stables. His three brothers suffered nothing and were as healthy as the day they came up from Devon. But not Tinker. Now, because of the foot-and-mouth order it looked as though he would have to stay in the Midlands and die.

'More gin,' ordered the Baroness curtly. And then, 'Listen to me.'

We all did, for obviously the Baroness had something up his sleeve. Every man-jack of us would have done anything just then for Mrs. W.J.-S. She would cheerfully have died herself rather than leave the 'children'. We had watched her with them for nine weeks thinking it rather a joke and failing to see her strength. Only she could drive Cinderella's coach. The ponies would obey none other—though Mrs. W.J.-S. did have the heaviest face disguise of anyone in the cast. She had been terrified of her former parlourmaid, who came from the Midlands, being in the audience and recognising her.

'I have a plan,' announced the Baroness.

It was simple. His family had come up in the caravan for the end of the panto's run.

'Recipe,' started the Baroness, 'take one caravan. Tip out one family. Put in one sick donkey ... '

'Pony,' interrupted Jack Frost.

'Tinker,' said Mrs. W.J.-S. to be precise.

'As I was saying,' repeated the Baroness, 'put in one sick animal. Take caravan plus sick animal to Devon. Return here with one healthy substitute animal from green fields of Devon. Tinker saved. Mother happy. Ministry Inspector satisfied on next inspection.'

It was a charmer of a plan. We put it into operation at once. It meant sitting up at the *Fox and Grapes* until seven in the morning waiting for Mrs. W.J.-S. to phone from Devon to say that all was well, though Jack Frost got through the last of his sequins long before then.

'My costume for next year,' he said proudly to the landlady who came down at three o'clock to make tea.

'I can't think what you're all up to at this hour,' she said suspiciously, eyeing the poor business manager in his green nylons sitting over the last of the fire.

So, you see, as I said at the beginning, don't try and tell *me* about pantomime in the Midlands. Of course, I went back the following year for more of it, and it was different again ... Yes, I'll have that pint.

L'Après-midi d'un Faune

YOU WOULD NOT HAVE THOUGHT IT possible for Victor to be such a happy little boy. He hardly ever found time to go frog-hunting in the Bog Meadows, and never in his whole life had he been to the Saturday morning cinema. Indeed, Saturday was the busiest day of a busy week, and his happiest. With the school closed he could look forward to the enjoyment of two whole days in the church. Victor's dad was sexton, kingpin of church affairs.

The keys lived in their house. Those from the parochial hall hung on a special hook on the dresser, while the most holy of all the keys, that for the church itself, lay hidden safely in the glory-hole under the stairs. This was a big key and heavy, with an ornamental head and a thick complicated end. It could be surrendered to no one, no matter who might call at the house, unless it was the curate perhaps, or the rector's warden. It alone among all the keys could turn the lock and give access through the great church door, where even bishops had sometimes to knock before it was opened unto them.

But much more than the opening of doors was involved. Being a large working-class parish the children always arrived early for Sunday school. They made a beeline for the piano and would pound its yellow notes unmercifully if Victor had forgotten to lock it until the arrival of Mrs. Parrot, the superintendent. There had been a terrible scene once when the rector walked in and found a crowd of the young rascals dropping *Golden Bells* through the lid while one of them vamped 'I can wash my daddy's shirt'.

Possession of the keys was an honour, their use a ritual, and the whole business surrounded by an air of privilege like some medieval ceremony. But the keys were more than the insignia of high office, for besides getting the place opened for the Sunday rush, the sexton had also to prepare the hall and church. From his earliest years Victor had helped his dad. By the time he reached ten he could be trusted to do certain jobs entirely on his own.

The pixie-ring of chairs used by the Mothers' Union, for instance, was one of his concerns. He had to move the chairs to one side, leaving a space for the G.F.S. gym class. This fell on Wednesdays and Victor ran all the way home from school, so that he could get to the red tin hall before the tea cooled in the copper urn. He locked himself in the hall, which still bore the faint scents of the afternoon's female occupation. Sitting on one of the chairs in the ring Victor would drink as many as six cups of tea and eat as much barm brack as the ladies had left. To warm his hands he would hold the cup and swing his legs to and fro, and study the bare hall which was his kingdom for an hour. The place was subject to his rule, he could order it according to his slightest whim. The curtains could be opened or closed, the drab green curtain masking the small stage could be drawn or folded back, the baize-covered card tables could be stood up or collapsed, the electric lights could be put on or off. All belonged to his jurisdiction, and as long as the chairs were ranged ready for the G.F.S. he could do as he pleased.

Although Wednesday was such a good day, Saturday was even better, for then his dad came with him. By ten o'clock they were there, breathing the familiar dry, dusty wooden smell that was different in winter when the gas radiators were lit, and as different again from the damp fungus smell of the neo-Gothic church hard by the hall. First the two of them stacked the chairs in twos round the walls, standing one upside down on the other so that they looked like impossible crabs with legs sticking helplessly in the air.

Then Victor went to the tiny kitchen, half-filled a bucket and went over the floor sprinkling water to lay the dust. He thought then of himself as being the sower he had seen in the Bible picture scattering seed by hand. Sometimes due to his imaginings Victor would take longer and be more thorough than the job strictly demanded, and then his dad would call him to speed up a bit. After the water came the sweeping. They both took brooms and started at one end, rolling before them the curious brown dirt that ingrained itself from Saturday to Saturday into the bare floorboards. Then they got the chairs again and set them in ten pixie-rings for the Sunday school classes, with a big one on the platform for the Young Men's Bible Class. Putting the chairs out was not as simple as it might sound. For one thing the teachers had their idiosyncrasies which must be catered for if wholesale rearrangement on Sunday afternoon was to be avoided. Some of the lady teachers did not like to sit too near radiators or underneath draughty windows while some of the men teachers wanted to be near the door so that they could slip out at the end for a quick smoke. And for another thing Victor remembered the exact number of chairs required for each class, and this too was quite a feat.

By Saturday midday the parish hall was as spick and span as broom and dustpan could make it. Victor and his dad went home for their dinner to prepare themselves for the day's major operation, the cleaning of the church during the afternoon. Here they were joined by his mother armed with a clump of feathers on the end of a bamboo stick for the woman's work of dusting. Victor had specific tasks which grew in degree of responsibility as he grew older. On Thursday night he had to lock the church after choir practice, first making sure that all the lights were switched off. On his way out he collected a slip of paper and put it in his pocket. This bore the coming Sunday's hymn numbers, and on Saturday afternoon it told him which numbers to display on the hymnboards. So that he could reach the slotted boards he took a chair, and the shoebox which contained the number cards, and went round the church putting up the hymns for morning worship.

Victor took as much care over the hymn numbers as Pythagoras did over the square of the hypotenuse. And when finished he stood back to admire his handiwork as proud as any Michelangelo of a Sistine ceiling. But greater visual delights than the puritan-looking black and white hymn numbers awaited him and this was the wicked splendour of the eagle-cock lectern. The proud brass bird had a cruel beak and stern expression which quite contradicted the theological notions of mercy and forgiveness. The vicious claws and the rich texture of his brass founder's feathers equally belied the Christian virtues of love and humility. And when he shone, after a liberal and vigorous application of Brasso and the remains of an old pair of coms, his glory was terrifying to see, a more wondrous spectacle than ever Aaron's golden calf could have been.

Then Victor's attentions were required in the pulpit, although here was something that irked his sense of order and his ideas about economy of effort. On the shelf immediately below the ledge which preachers thumped to gain their effect, stood a carafe of water. Unlike the mission hall sermonisers, the church clergy never drank during sermons. But Victor did wish they would use the water sometimes. When he took up the carafe and peered into it like a crystal gazer looking for signs and portents, he saw nothing but thousands of tiny bubbles which had grown on the sides since the previous Sunday. It seemed such a waste of care and thoughtfulness to renew the water week by week knowing that it would never be used. Sometimes he had hopes that a choir lady would fall down in a dead faint during one of the longer and more tedious hymns, so that he could dash up the aisle from the sexton's pew, leap into the pulpit and bring out the carafe, and by reviving the victim become the hero of the hour. But nothing so dramatic

ever happened, and the most to be hoped for was one of
Councillor Crum's coughing attacks which obliged this red-faced
gas victim of the First World War to leave the church, strangely
enough, often just before the sermon.

By the time the carafe was replaced, the black heating pipes
which snaked by the walls and along the ends of the pews began
to emit loud percussive sounds as though some desperate
creature was trapped inside and was trying to escape. But it was
only Victor's dad down in the boiler house lighting up the fire
that must be kept going until Sunday evening. Victor had no
time to go down the broken steps from the churchyard to see the
size of last week's clinkers which were being raked out. He loved
the fused misshapen lumps and knew that any outstanding
specimens would be taken home by his dad for making the path
to their railway allotment. But usually when the raking began
Victor was already on holy ground behind the communion rails
putting golden-fringed markers in at the collects and epistles.
And because by now he could decipher the Table of Lessons he
stood on the wooden box behind the lectern and placed not-so-
ornate markers in the vast Bible which rested on the eagle-
cock's outspread wings.

And then finally Victor went to a cupboard in the vestry. He
saved the best of all the jobs until the end, making a grand
climax. And here he was entirely his own master and more, for
in his hands rested the possible saving of souls. It was in no
frivolous state of mind that he approached the task of renewing
the message in the wayside pulpit. The wooden frame stood just
behind the churchyard wall on the opposite side of the gate from
the noticeboard with its gilt lettering giving times of the
services. The wayside pulpit was sadly in need of paint and its
joints were rickety with age. But at least in this it could proclaim
poverty and the blessings which belonged to the poor. And
anyway, people were meant to read the poster he pinned up and
not waste time admiring the frame. The posters were displayed
for a week and the selection of them was Victor's responsibility.
A roll of texts was kept in the vestry cupboard and it was there

that Victor repaired just as Saturday dusk fell. Choose the hymns and psalms he could not, but the scriptural quotations in bold type were entirely his affair. Victor knew well the power of the printed word and felt sure that it would not return void unto its Author. Moreover, the wayside pulpit stood in an ideally strategic position by the penny fare stage. The shipyard workers queued there and as nothing else around vied for their attention he hoped they learned the texts by heart. Victor would have been surprised had he realised how few of the shipyard men noticed that the wayside pulpit existed.

At last all was ready for Sunday dawn, ready for the worshipper who would file into the church, oblivious of the work behind the scenes, ready for the hordes of children whose parents wanted them out of the way after the week's biggest meal so that they could relax or get the bed to themselves. All that was left for Victor to do was to prepare himself and this he did by the regular Saturday night bath in front of the kitchen fire. As soon as he sank into the water Victor realised how tired the day's exertions had made him. But it was the pleasant tiredness of work well done. He would sleep then in his small iron bed upstairs, happy to know that he would wake to the Lord's Day clean in body and soul (for he always said his prayers before getting into bed) ready to put on his Sunday clothes. Waiting for him was a navy-blue suit, white shirt and red-striped tie. The black shoes still had the stiffness of being new because they were only worn once a week, but the polish on them rivalled that of the eagle-cock in the church. Victor felt that his own person was the finishing touch, the final flourish which assured that Sunday would be a success.

It always was. He spent the whole day in church, even the afternoons. Because it was a poor parish there were plenty of christenings to fill in the early afternoon gap between morning service and Sunday school, with sometimes a small present for himself, as it was he who filled the font from the churchyard watering can and got the register out of the solemn safe. Although the whole of Sunday was a sparkling day its sparkling highlight came with the evening service. To begin with the congregation was larger than the mornings. This thrilled Victor for he regarded the parishioners not as members of the body of Christ but as an audience. From his point of view they came to see the spectacular display put on by him and his dad and, of course, the rector and the curates. They did not actually pay to come in but nevertheless expected some sort of a show. The scene had been carefully and lovingly set on Saturday and the players appeared on stage with a special glory. His dad filled a principal role dressed for the occasion in his long black gown. Not even the clergy had velvet on their robes, and only the bishop himself carried anything remotely like his dad's wand of office.

Before the service began, Victor stood with his dad, who was always dignified by his gown, and together they handed out the neat pairs of books, one *Church Hymnal* and one *Common Prayer*. Parish magazines once a month were handed out in packets to the lady distributors, or individual copies sold to those not on the list of regular subscribers.

Nobody who knew the church well, or even strangers for that matter, could make any mistake about Victor's importance. Indeed, in conversation, he and his dad were often linked so that on mentioning the sexton people automatically added 'and Victor' or 'and his lad'. Sometimes when the rector made arrangements for midweek meetings in the church hall, he would simply say 'and put out chairs for fifty people, Victor'. And often the magazine secretary would ask him, 'Did Mrs. Cooke pick up her packet last week?' or, 'I've forgotten how many magazines Mrs. Butler takes'.

Victor could always answer. He knew not only about magazine packets, but about free-will offering envelopes too. The modest anonymity of the little envelopes did not fool him, his eyes penetrated like X-rays and he could tell who left the fattest ones and how much they contained. From the time the rector appeared at the vestry door and announced the opening hymn until he climbed into the pulpit for the sermon Victor had nothing to do. In that split second came the most exciting time of all. Victor again was involved in the performance, in moulding the audience for the next part of the drama. As in a theatre, the lights were lowered so that all attention should be focused on the pulpit. As soon as the rector started to pray during the last verse of the pre-sermon hymn Victor stole out unobserved to the switch cupboard, to turn off the nave lamps. Skill was required if the people were not to be distracted by the wrong ones being switched off and then on again, or dazzled by any other switchboard mishaps. And he had to remember exactly the reverse process when the rector ended his sermon and the people stood up for 'God the Father, God the Son and God the Holy Ghost'.

For Victor the apex of this whole structure of weekend delights was the taking up of the collection. It was the Grand March of his *Aida*, the Act III of his *Meistersinger*, the final scene of his *Zauberflöte*. With a tinkling and a jingling hardly drowned by the post-sermon hymn, the collection plates went along the rows of pews, passing to and fro like a weaver's shuttle. Then with military precision a procession formed in the centre aisle at the back. At its head, like a general in front of his army, stood Victor's dad. Victor could not resist turning round to see the start of the not-too-slow, not-too-quick march to the communion rail. He swivelled his head following them right up the church. The curate received the money plates on the large brass platter, and then in turn handed it to the rector. He in his turn offered it to God, with his arms fully stretched straight above his head holding the plate as though he could almost but not quite reach the hands of angels leaning down to take the money up to heaven.

Victor understood, of course, that this was a symbolic act, but he had never quite recovered from the shock of the first time he had ever gone into the vestry immediately after the evening service. There on the baize tablecloth was all the money spread out being raked over by the wardens and put into little linen oatmeal sacks. It had seemed a most unholy thing, to count and handle these very special coins which had already been up to heaven. But Victor was a sensible lad and understood that while they had not exactly pretended to give the money to God, the facts were that the rector and his churchwardens had to use it on God's behalf. And Victor though how wonderful it would be to go into a shop and buy a tin of polish for the eagle-cock, 'Can I have a tin of Brasso for God, please?' But for some reason or other, the church people didn't even do this.

But in spite of these difficulties, the presentation of the money at the altar was a solemn occasion, followed at once by the procession's return. The sidesmen did a smart about-turn, Victor's dad neatly took up the leading position again. What a magnificent figure he was, with all eyes fastened on him. The wand was held with an authority that all the years of usage had taught him. He walked with the dignity and assurance learnt as a drum-boy in the Irish Guards. The black gown hung open at the front just enough to expose the twin loops of gold watch chain festooned across his belly like Baroque swags. The sexton held his head high and proudly, looking as though the come-to-Jesus collar was made of steel preventing him even from giving a blink of the eyes. Victor had never had any ambition to be an engine driver or a submarine sailor, he wanted only one thing when he grew up and that was to be sexton like his dad, master of ceremonies, man of the hour.

Being grown up seemed a long way away, yet in no time Victor was past his twelfth birthday and already a lance-corporal in the C.L.B. And it was about then that Victor and the Devil became mutually aware of each other, an association not without fascination. Victor's birthday was followed by a full-blooded spring which gave way to a stifling summer. The sultry weather called a response within Victor himself. The energy stoked up inside his vigorous body seemed as stifling as the weather, for nothing he did seemed to quench it. No sooner had he done one job than he was ready for another. No number of journeys running from home to the parish hall abated his strength, no amount of chair stacking or pulling bell ropes, which he had learned to do, could exhaust him. The sun burned down on the hall's tin roof, transforming the inside into an oven, where Victor and his dad sweated over their brooms, choked with the dust that rose up like a pestilence, despite heavy sprinklings of water. Yet Victor came out of the hall fresher than before going in.

The Devil could see what a stout soul he was up against in young Victor. Few fully-fledged church members, let alone boys, were as zealous in church work. And what boy could the Devil spy on and find spending patient hours on the repair of torn hymn-books or Bible pages? How many young men of twelve years could be left entirely alone in the church full of harvest festival bounty without taking a single apple or even a grape from the cornucopia of gifts strewn on every ledge and niche? Only Victor did deeds of this calibre, knowing that no mortal eyes watched, only the unsleeping ones of his Maker and those of the Father of Lies.

Without stretching imagination too far Victor could now think of himself as a proper sexton. The school holiday was for six weeks and, taking advantage of this, his dad was hard at work putting their railway allotment into good shape. A multitude of church jobs were left to Victor and all the usual daily running of errands. When he was not at the hall or in the church, Victor stayed near the house for the callers on church business occupied his whole day. Most of them entailed the carrying of a message through the parish's endless rows of Victorian slum houses. The rector and two curates were, so Victor believed, run off their feet trying to cover the acres of narrow streets over which their care of souls extended. Hospitals and workhouse, cemetery and rectory all had to be connected by a network of errands for which only the willing Victor seemed to be available. There were marriages and christenings, the Sunday school outings and C.L.B. camps all to be organised and which all seemed to be susceptible to last minute hitches. And the uncustomary heat was knocking the old people down like flies. Victor failed to understand why so many urgent messages were left at his house concerning the aged, for he was bursting with wellbeing. He kept constantly in his mind the last nature lesson in school.

Something of the sort, he felt, was happening to him. The sun that stood so starkly in the sky each morning was baking him from a chrysalis into a brilliant dragonfly. He could not see why anyone should want to die when living was so good.

But it was a call from the dying which sent Victor scurrying to find the new curate. First he went to the allotment to ask his dad for the address. But as the sexton could not remember, Victor raced to the church noticeboard where it stood out in bold new letters. Victor did not altogether trust or approve of curates. They were fly-by-nights, the tinkers of the clergy, here today and gone tomorrow. Their names were always in new paint, unlike the rector's and his dad's which had been painted so long ago that they were almost illegible, a sign of permanence like that of the equally faded times of the services. Since everyone knew perfectly well where the rectory and sexton's house were, the painted names were pointless anyway. In Victor's mind it was something of a condemnation that curates possessed identity only in as far as the noticeboard gave it to them.

Such thoughts occupied him as he hurried to the new curate's house, having the address printed on his memory. Victor hurried so much that he was conscious of little but the heat beating down from the sun and the tar on the road which was breaking into bubbles. The sun scorched his neck and because he had his old worn-out gutties on and no stockings he could feel the hot tar through the holes. Each time he put his foot down, the tar sank a little, stung him like a jellyfish, and was reluctant to let the sole free again. Several times Victor paused to see if he pressed his foot hard, whether the tar would seriously burn him through the holes in his gutties. He knew that he dare not arrive at the curate's house with his gutties hanging by their laces round his neck. He went barefoot like this on his rare outings to the Bog Meadows, or when he went alone to the allotment, enjoying the same freedom as the tinker children who lived in rag tents. But a budding sexton could hardly behave in this way, at any rate, not in the streets where he would be seen.

And it was precisely at this juncture that the Devil began

operations against Victor. Being only a boy, and a church boy at that, Victor's notion of sin was simple. It just consisted of a list containing certain deeds which were forbidden. If you did anything on the list, sin was committed. Victor had no idea that the serpent was the most subtle of all the field's beasts. And now because in admitting that an assistant sexton should not be seen *in public* with his gutties off, but that in private it was all right, Victor was falling into the easiest sin of all—the lie of respectability. After all, looked at in one way, the worst aspect of Adam and Eve's sin in the Garden was that they tried afterwards to pretend that nothing had happened. All unconscious that he had given the Devil an opening, Victor had allowed now that he could do things in private which would never be known in public. If those things were not on the sin list then all was well but if they were he would be in jeopardy.

Innocent of the gulf opening at his feet, Victor rang the bell which hung in the porch of the big posh house, where the curate was lodging. A maid opened the door, emitting a smell of polish which she continued to apply after showing Victor in. The curate, it appeared, was playing tennis. This was a shock to Victor who had never come across a tennis-playing curate before. In general, curates were notoriously unsportsmanlike. The most they ever did was to start the three-legged race at the C.L.B. sports.

The maid was unimpressed when Victor explained who he was. Without saying one word she managed to convey the impression that sextons, let alone their sons, were not a class of person with whom she was accustomed to dealing. And she clearly did not trust Victor—he who held the keys to the sliver chalice, the eagle-cock and goodness knows how many missionary boxes. True she allowed him into the hall, but instead of discreetly retiring as she would have done with any other visitor, she hovered about the fringes, dusting this, straightening that and giving unnecessary rubbings to things already brightly polished. Victor was uncomfortable, and instinctively knew that the maid had him under observation yet

without looking at him. She began to dust the stairs, starting at
the top, working downwards. All Victor could see now was more
of her garters and thighs than was good for Christian eyes.

Victor, however, was in a predicament for where else could he
look? Certainly not at the hall table for there stood a statue of
the Devil himself, laughing and giving naughty looks with his
eyes. Victor had no doubt that it was the Devil, for unlike statues
in the museum it had no fig leaf and was the only one he had
ever seen with Old Nick's tail. Victor could not understand why
the curate went on living in such a worldly house. Little wonder
he played tennis.

Down the stairs came the maid, one at a time, flicking her
duster in and out like a snake's tongue, until she reached the last
tread and the grey blancmanges of her thighs were under cover.
Then she began to dust the ornate table which served as the
Devil-statue's altar. Victor tried not to look. But the strange
figure hypnotised him. Then she did it. Yes, she wiped the
bronze body, *all* over. From deep down a blush rose and flushed
Victor's face to the deepest scarlet. He could not help it, even
though the maid had turned to look at him. Observing his
embarrassment she gave him a wink, not the quick saucy one of
the girls in the street, but a wink full of wickedness and meaning.
Nakedness, Victor knew, was the most terrible thing in the
whole world. That was why God went about in a flowing
nightshirt that covered his ankles, while the Devil did not have
a single stitch to his buff. And naturally all those hundreds of
pennies and thousands of halfpennies went into the missionary
boxes in order to clothe the nakedness of the poor heathen.
Only the week before school closed for the holidays a boy in
Victor's class had been caned and sent home for having a gaping
rent in the seat of his trousers.

Having devastated Victor's sense of modesty, the maid
collected her dusters and went into the back garden to hurry the
curate from the tennis court. Alone and confronted by the
Devil, Victor's resistance collapsed and he went over to examine
the statue. Every detail confirmed that it was indeed Old Nick,

for of course Victor could not be expected to recognise the Dancing Faun of Pompeii when he saw it. Throwing Christian principle to the winds, instead of taking a rose petal from a nearby bowl and giving it a museum costume, he stroked it. What a fantastic dance the figure was doing and what reckless enjoyment beamed on its pleasantly mischievous face, what vitality and abandonment seemed to vibrate in those limbs and muscular shoulders. A voice somewhere inside Victor struggled to be heard and it said how wonderful it would be if Victor threw off all his clothes and pranced about like that. But this voice was quickly drowned by an even stronger one which had the most wicked thing to say that could ever be said or even thought of by any human being. And it was this, that plain evidence showed that the Devil was a much more inviting and intriguing person that the dreary old Godhead in His yards and yards of white linen. Victor looked again at the statue and saw that even its tail was rather cute and not the terrifying mark of evil that he would have expected.

What with the two voices inside him, and certain things that now emerged from his mind, Victor began to realise that, far from being the spotless servant of God like the boy Samuel, he had already had some considerable liaison with the Devil over this question of nakedness. It had begun, he supposed, with the taking off his gutties as soon as he got to the railway allotments. The queer, unidentified sensation of walking about on freshly turned soil, or feeling the leaves gently stroke his bare legs as he picked peas, was extremely gratifying. But better still were the Saturday night baths. If alone in the house, he would go upstairs and dry himself in front of the big mirror on the wardrobe door. He relished the sight of his own body and bent his arms to see if the biceps were forming or if manly pectorals were forming on his chest, the kind of he-man bodies possessed by saints undergoing martyrdom in the church's stained-glass windows. And what of his behaviour during the suffocating nights of that very summer? There had hardly been one when he had not slept naked on, not in, his bed. Admittedly, he did not remove his shirt until after saying his prayers, for to have prayed in the nude would really have insulted his Maker. This would have been a much worse sin than even peeing in the entry or robbing the gas meter which a lot of boys at school did. Any further speculation was cut short by the arrival of the breathless, sweating curate who, to Victor's astonishment, was wearing white shorts. Victor had never seen such a thatch of hairs on anyone's legs before, though the curate did not look that strong. He had another quarter of an hour to reflect on this last shock while the curate flitted away upstairs to change and get himself in a fit state to carry comfort to the dying.

Victor was surprised, though not at all displeased, to discover that he could not rid himself of the statue. An image of its face grinned at him everywhere, even in church. To fight this lurking Satan, he closed his eyes and tried to think hard of God's shiny, dazzling robes that blazed the sky with lightning when he grew angry, as He certainly would if He knew Victor's thoughts. But as soon as he stopped thinking about God, the dancing Devil came back, darting about like spots before the eyes. The Devil even preceded Victor's dad in the collection procession, wagging his little tail affectionately, and giving the naughtiest looks imaginable at the rectory pew and blowing wicked kisses at the two Misses Greenhorns who were so rich that they gave the C.L.B.s annual efficiency cup. Victor could not drive out the Devil so he gave up trying to and in the end also gave up wanting to. For he had come to admit to himself that the statue symbolised so many of his own secret pleasures. Would he ever become so wicked, Victor wondered, as to spend Sunday mornings in bed with the *News of the World*, as so many of their neighbours did?

The situation was not improved by the weather. Hot day succeeded hot day, long, languishing heat-drenched hours, in which the sun was a white-hot crucible pouring down molten light. All kinds of strange feelings stirred in Victor. Spending so much time alone in the parish hall left the way open for temptation, which fell on him like showers of arrows. It drove

Victor berserk and one day he went as far as to get the bottle of sacramental wine to see if it really did taste like blood. Whether it was like other people's blood he could not tell but it was certainly not like his own, for he always sucked a cut finger, and so he knew. But then, he was certain by now that his body was different from others, like those of the tomb-dwellers of Gergesenes, possessed of devils. Things had to come to a climax soon, or he would burst.

Victor began to find that his usual world was no longer big enough to contain him. He noticed, as if for the first time, how small their house was, how narrow its street, how dingy the parish hall. Even the church lost its awe-inspiring aspect. Its loftiness became foreshortened, the mystery of its nave and sanctuary shrank to mere clammy gloom, striking him less pleasantly than the fine summer afternoon outside. And his usual inclination to dress up in his dad's robe did not worry him. It was too wonderful outside to be bothered with ushering imaginary sidesmen up to the communion rail, rehearsing and training for the day when he would be sexton. Even in the church Victor felt hot and, standing though he was polishing the eagle-cock, he wanted to follow the Devil and fling off his gutties and shirt. Had some heroic deed needed to be done Victor felt as though he could do it. If a sailing ship had come proudly into the Belfast roads, Victor thought he would have run away to sea. But there seemed no way at all in which he could break free. The C.L.B. camp was the event most likely to provide the thrill he needed but it still lay two weeks away, and even then would not satisfy him.

Suddenly he realised his terrible handicap in being only twelve years and a half old. Nobody took him seriously. All the church people he dealt with, from the rector to the magazine ladies, from the organist to the youngest child in the Sunday school thought of him as the sexton's son. He was the boy who helped clean the church and who ran errands to the parish's furthest houses, who was *such* a help to his dad and the dear rector. None of them, Victor realised, ever thought that he had a life of his own, an existence quite separate from the church. None would have the wit to imagine that he had an interior life different from his official one. Did they think, he inquired angrily of himself, that he wanted to spend all his life carrying their messages, sweeping their floors, setting out chairs for their silly meetings? Big, noble, brave things awaited him on the high seas wrestling with taut canvas in gales, or swinging from tree to tree in jungles as mad savages pursued him. Victor did not remember in such strained moments that only a few months previously they had been *God's* errands, chairs and meetings. Discontent seemed inevitable. But it was also urgent and vital, and the only thing which could carry him through the summer. He was deeply disturbed but nothing could be done. Victor could neither douse the flames of restlessness nor let them utterly consume him.

For the first time in his life Victor's dad began to speak sharply to him. In the parish hall and church jobs Victor's preoccupations made him careless and things well done before were now badly done or left unfinished. At home his former willingness to help alternated between a surly laziness and fierce demands that the whole place be turned upside down to suit his own ideas. The sexton was more perplexed than angry at his son's changed behaviour. He was too proud a man to confide his worries to the rector. He thought it was his responsibility as a father to control his son. He reckoned that he knew all there was to know about discipline having spent his adolescence in the Irish Guards. So the sexton took himself off early to the allotment, thinking that a long school holiday was all very well but the children got out of hand for want of things to do.

Although keen enjoyment had gone from his church activities, Victor could not leave the place alone. It was the only anchor he had, the only place where he could find rhythm in the wild off beat of his life. So on Wednesdays he went as usual to the parish hall to clear up after the Mothers' Union. Not having had school, Victor set off early one afternoon, taking his time and arriving at the hall before the women had finished. He

peered through a crack in the doors and saw the plates of barm
brack and Devon splits which would be left for him when they
had gone. Because of the holidays and the unbroken weather,
Victor calculated, many of the mothers must have gone away
down to Bangor on excursions, so there would be plenty of food
left over. He could just hear the secretary uttering the closing
prayer, and he wished she would hurry up and get out.

At last he had the hall to himself. Giving people his usual
cheery smiles and remarks was becoming daily more difficult.
But he managed not to offend the women and locked the doors
behind the last of them. It was still mid-afternoon. The hall
baked in the heat, its tin roof creaking occasionally as though
the heat was too much for it. A sense of closure and isolation
possessed Victor as he swallowed cups of sweet tea. It was an
exciting, tense atmosphere transforming his ordinary sense of
mastery over the hall into a desire for domination. He felt as
though he could do anything, though he could think of nothing
to do. Perhaps he could play about on the gym apparatus when
he cleared the ring of chairs and set up the equipment for the
G.F.S. This idea seemed to have possibilities of rescuing his
afternoon from frustration and boredom, so leaving some cakes
until later he set about the hall.

A queer sense of apprehension seized him as he cleared the
chairs and dragged the gym apparatus across the floor. It made
him sweat and he longed to be out in the Bog Meadows jumping
sheughs or lying among cool rushes. Not being free to leave his
work without risk of another row at home and without upsetting
the evening's G.F.S., Victor decided on the next best thing. He
kicked the gutties from his feet and took his shirt off. Suddenly
he felt like a hero about to conquer. With his mind full of
fanciful situations which could embroil a hero, Victor ran at the
wooden horse and vaulted it, and then swung for minutes on end
on the parallel bars. He became aware of the bittersweet smell of
his own sweat and this spurred him to further violent movement.
The strength of his body amazed him. Victor felt that the way
his fingers gripped the bars, the way the muscles in his upper

arms and shoulders were strong enough to hold him, showed that it would not be long before he became a man.

Leaving the parallel bars Victor ran to the section of wall bars at one end of the hall. He never realised before how the gym apparatus made him as flexible as rubber, as tough as steel, and enabled his body to do so many things, running, leaping and climbing. On the wall bars fantastic exercises could be done. The cold, hard wood pressing against his naked upper body stirred him in a peculiar way. It was as though his body reached out to embrace all things around it, to feel sensuously the reality of their existence. Before his mind now passed a cavalcade of sensations that his body loved. There was the hardness of stone and iron which he could feel when leaning over the parapet of railway bridges, and the wood he felt on the wall bars. These hard things sought out the bones under his muscles and skin, hardness responded to hardness. But when he lay sunbathing in the Bog Meadows it was the velvet scrape of grass against his skin which was wonderful, just as the sheets seemed to stroke him when he slipped into bed without his shirt. His clothes and gutties had a special quality too, as though they were part of his body, an extra skin put off and on night and morning, with its own familiar touch and smell.

But these feelings had never pressed round him so strongly as on that hot afternoon in the airless hall. The windows, the dusty boarded floor, the tin walls and the rafters seemed to be closing in on him, demanding response, demanding an affirmation of energy that leapt within him. This overwhelmed Victor as he ran from the wall bars and shinned up one of the climbing ropes. He had done it a hundred times before in C.L.B. meetings, but the rope never seemed alive before in quite the same way. He had never noticed the rope's solid roundness before, nor the way its coils pressed into his palms. When he reached the top Victor clung to the hook which held the rope. His head touched the high ceiling. And as he hung there like a swallow under the eaves, a stupendous sensation swept over him. It swamped him like a wave, and covered him like sea water with a tingling and stinging of his whole body so that for a moment he could neither see nor hear, and then retreated, leaving behind trails of sweetness, which ebbed slowly away.

Hardly able to tell whether it had all been imagination or had actually happened, Victor climbed quickly down the rope exultant at this new experience. A relaxation possessed him, though his strength was undiminished. Then unbidden into his mind came the truth, the stark and horrible truth about what had just happened to him. Far from being transported to paradise he had sunk to the depths of hell. The few seconds of ineffable bliss were damnation. Victor realised that he had done what boys in school were always talking about. Firing, they called it.

Alarmed at his wickedness, Victor struggled into his shirt and made for the door. The lock stuck and he panicked, thinking that he was trapped and would be discovered in his guilt. But the key turned and he was out, with only a backward glance at the hanging rope, whose end was exactly like the statue's tail in the curate's house. Without stopping Victor led through the streets, over the pavements, down entries, fighting his way towards the wide steppes of the Bog Meadows. And when the grass underfoot replaced cobbles and paving stones, he ran on, not slowing until the Blackstaff was crossed by the stepping stones and he was far from the tinkers' tents and grazing piebalds.

Exhausted by the run he flung himself desperately on the ground. He was surprised to find himself still alive. At every step of the way he had been expecting a thunderbolt to pierce his shoulder blades, flung by an outraged God from heaven. Well, that at least hasn't happened, he thought ruefully, lying face down because he dared not turn to the sky in case the flushed, angry eyes of God should look at him. Perhaps God had not found out yet. There might be a chance of hiding the whole thing, of ridding himself of this dangerous alliance with the dancing Devil. Some way must exist for draining badness out of himself. Should he go and lie in one of the sheughs full of leeches? A boy in school stuck a leech on a black eye he got in a fight. He claimed the leech could draw out all the bad juices.

What horror Victor had of leeches, yet he would do it if he could save himself. A heaviness entered his body now. The late afternoon sun caressed him. A reckless unconcern stole over him. Let God kill me if He wants to, he thought and then fell asleep.

When he woke, to find himself whole and undamaged by either God or the Devil, he became bold, and laughed at his own cringing cowardice. So far as he could tell the rest of the world had not changed. He could see the factory chimneys smoking over the city, and clouds drifting over the mountains. In less than an hour the G.F.S. would go to the parish hall to find it locked if he were not there. Victor no longer felt the resentment against all the people who expected so much from him. He thought of the girls in their gym tunics. Some of them made it plain that they liked him, and he would hate himself more for spoiling their evening than ever he did for the events earlier in the afternoon. In fact he did not hate himself even for that. After all, the other boys at school did it.

But more than anything at the moment Victor wanted something to eat. He remembered the pieces of barm brack left in the hall. If he got there before the girls he could wolf it all. When he arrived out of breath from running again, he fell ravenously on the thick pieces, wondering when he had ever been so hungry. He eyed the climbing rope, hanging suggestively, like a jungle liana that no Tarzan could resist. Victor wondered whether if he climbed it again, the miraculous sensation would be as beautiful as it was the first time.

It was.

Still Waters

IN THE DAYS BEFORE THE SECOND World War trains still ran to Enniskillen and only the travelling grocer brought wonders of the motor age to Tullyreen's laneways. Church and chapel had, it is true, closed their gates on the last horse trap when leggings came off and cycle clips went on. And nobody thereabouts felt more pride in her Rudge than did Kate Lyttle who on a January morning dismounted at the church gate from the high saddle of her Christmas-new bicycle and leant it against a headstone to rest.

With a growing family of six and Enniskillen's drapery shops as many miles away, the Rudge released Kate from waiting to see whether the travelling grocer had brought by luck, the right-sized boots among the dehorning sticks and cudding powders. Nor did the Rudge's blessing fall on Kate alone. Pleasure flushed her husband Tom's handsome face twice a week when she spun into town with strings of rabbits on the handlebars. Proceeds from rabbits he trapped after work made possible more than Kate's shining machine. Having seen his father drink his way through two farms, Tom neither smoked or drank but spent his share of the rabbit funds on his camera.

Ever since the age of twelve and the first brownie bought with trading stamps Tom had viewed life through his camera lens. Marriage and the no less strenuous work at the creamery never obscured his boyhood love of fixing the beautiful moment forever in silver bromide. But Tom's delight in Kate's rabbit-laden expeditions to town, snapped two-score times if once by him, was not a delight Kate felt towards his camera and its results. Even though her mother assured her Tom gave less in a month for film than most men spent in a week on drink, Kate still thought it all a waste of good money, particularly, as she was never slow to point out, not a single entry of his in newspaper competitions had ever appeared in print. This lack of public evidence in what she termed 'black and white' (a harsh assessment of Tom's devotion to the subtle arts of *chiaroscuro*) accompanied a similar lack of private display. She regarded his efforts in such a poor light that a ban on the snapshots even excluded them from the mantlepiece. In the end Tom concealed not only his wounded pride but his pictures also. Kate was never shown the latest films.

Though Tom's was doubtless not the first camera ever to be the occasion if not the cause of dissension in a marriage, his enjoyed a unique marital position at least in Tullyreen. Many a sharp word and sharper riposte flew to and fro when Tom commandeered the scullery as a darkroom. Whole evenings passed when Kate scolded in vain for him to replenish the turf basket or fetch a bucket of water. But stronger tides pulled below the choppy surface. The latest Kodak roused passions of jealousy. For three Sundays in a row Tom disappeared with his treasure without dropping so much as a copper in the church plate. Instinct made Kate too clever to question her man on his wanderings, but she seldom missed the opportunity of squinting at the negatives drying on the clothes line. Such a cut of a man was Tom that he had no need of a serge suit to show off his proud figure.

Kate struggled with her temper when Tom came home of a Sunday after midnight, for times were bad with the B-Specials on the roads. This was before the camera had a flashlight and who, thought Kate, could be taking pictures and it as dark as the inside of the sergeant's boot? Anger rising like milk on the boil, Kate threatened to bury the camera in the boghole. Next morning she saw the wisdom of her mother's 'take hold of yourself, Kate', though by then nothing could bring back the rush of abuse. Yet as she watched Tom take his midday piece off to the creamery Kate knew she was the only woman in the terrace whose man would return that night with no smell of drink taken. She could count the same blessing even at the end of their red-letter day—the annual charabanc outing to the Donegal Sea.

Neither Tom nor Kate asked for more excitement than this, at least, not until the new rector came from a Laganside curacy and turned their heads with the glories of Belfast. Then nothing could contain them until they clambered aboard the charabanc bound not for the Donegal Sea, but eastward for the city where the day's trip would take in no less than the Twelfth of July walk to Finaghy Field itself.

Loyalties divided Kate. Horizons beyond the range of her bicycle held few attractions. Also, she could not forget, whatever the splendours might be of Belfast's new parishes with no allocated sittings, that only last Twelfth the city streets had run with human blood. But in a place like Tullyreen a new rector with missionary zeal could move any mountain and not a vacant place could be seen in the bus nosing through the Fermanagh countryside to Belfast. Although the creamery manager sat in their midst, Tom appeared to be running the show, for not only had his neighbours proclaimed him official photographer but had presented him with no less than six reels of film on which to record the great day. What, in such circumstances, could Kate do but take her place by his side?

And of course the rector's prophecies all came true. Not only had the Tullyreen photographer and his wife never seen a town of such size but the whole Orange world had turned out to parade before their all but unbelieving eyes. Lambeggers whacked their fat drums, silver maces flashed in the summer air

above drum-majors leading accordion bands and pipers in kilts
still creased by the night journey from Scotland, silver
trumpeters in uniform each more gorgeous than the band before
were only the accompaniment to the thousands of brethren
marching in sashes and hard hats. Spotless white gloves gripped
menacing pikestaffs while young boys, like tugs round great ships
off Queen's Island, clutched at the thick Orange ropes securing
silken banners of 'Victoria giving a Blackamoor the secret of
England's Greatness' in the form of a Bible. There was Ruth the
Moabite, the death of Schomberg, there were Old Testament
prophets and World War I battle scenes. And everywhere were
dozens of banners depicting no less a person than King William
himself crossing Boyne water.

The six reels of film went in no time, yet hardly more than a
glimpse of the Twelfth's great throng seemed to have been
captured for the people of Tullyreen. In a trance, Kate handed
over two half-crowns from her personal savings to buy more
films. A third demand, however, dispelled the trance in a trice.
She put her foot down. The money was there all right, in the
back of her purse, but at the back of her mind was a new dynamo
lamp for her bicycle. And in any case, now that she had come to
her senses again, there was something disturbing about the
whole thing quite apart from the few shillings for the films.

They had now reached Finaghy Field and most of their
neighbours from Tullyreen scattered until the bus left at seven in
the evening. Although Tom went on photographing it was not
the Supreme Grand Mistress of the Bronx Prince of Orange or
the Detroit Defenders of the Faith who appeared in the
viewfinder. A band of girl pipers lay relaxing among the
haystacks. And when Kate returned with the second batch of
films it was not the Imperial Grand Master's speech on the
loudspeakers the girl pipers were cheering, but Tom's pranks,
which even an amateur could see were not part of any
photographic process.

Kate flared up but managed to take hold of herself despite the
added provocation of a Tullyreen neighbour who ensured she

should turn no blind eye on Tom's making a fool of himself. His third demand for film money following this mild flirtation met with a flood of invective, the general import of which was that while he might choose to make a fool of himself in public he was not going to make one of her. Kate flounced off, swearing to usurp that which the Secret of England's greatness reserved as a divine prerogative—vengeance. Hers was no slow and small grinding vengeance, however, but one which required immediate and violent outlet. Her hand went to her purse and came out again holding the money Tom had wanted for films and which in a minute lay in the hands of a stallholder who sold Kate a plate of split-devons and a bottle of sarsaparilla which washed the cream buns down. These gaudy luxuries, whose sole purpose was to squander on vanities the coins Tom needed for higher things, were no sooner consumed than pangs of remorse struck Kate rather worse than the pangs of indigestion a stomach unaccustomed to sarsaparilla was to give her almost simultaneously.

Two o'clock had barely gone. Five empty hours stretched ahead, without oasis, until seven when the charabanc should leave for Tullyreen. Not a half of these had passed before a subdued Kate was in the field looking for her man. But Tom was not to be found. Nor was there a sight of that particular tartan, to distinguish those particular girl pipers. Fear took the place of anger now and Kate called off her search of the hayfield and those adjoining and returned to the place where she had bought the two lots of film. Neither Tom nor any soul from Tullyreen was there. Although very distressed at being alone and worried both by the wantonness of the kilted girl pipers and her knowledge that Tom was born with a soft drop, Kate did not lose her head. Nor did the distress dull her countrywoman's senses. Her nose had caught the scent of a bargain not to be missed for she had seen how cheap the city films were compared with those bought at home from the rabbit proceeds. The day's outing took a large bite from the meagre cake of their savings, and Kate, who did the family budgeting, saw that bulk purchasing of film would repair some of the financial damage. She would lay in a supply of the cheap films against the weeks and months ahead, as she had never at any time expected to get the dynamo lamp before Christmas.

Confidence returned as Kate carried the bag of films. It laid balm on the wounds inflicted by the unfortunate events of the Twelfth outing and promised halcyon days thereafter when Kate would be sure that the handsome Tom Lyttle was safely ensconced in the scullery messing about with developing rather than messing about on the hill with other kinds of developing in some hussy's arms.

Kate followed people streaming back to Belfast. The Albert struck five o'clock before she spied anyone from Tullyreen, though she gave the neighbour a wide berth. The six cottages that formed the terrace at Tullyreen were far from substantial and no one kept a hen that crowed concealed for long. Tom and his wandering the countryside with a camera instead of a ferret box had given rise to enough speculation without the added ignominy of an open quarrel on the Twelfth of July at the big parade.

On that evening crowing, let alone plucking, was the last thing Kate wanted to do. Her hands sweated for reasons other than the late afternoon's humid heat or the tackiness of the paper bag with the films. As the Albert relentlessly struck the quarter-hours and hours away Kate lingered at the quayside, her mind haunted by the Big Boat and those whom Tullyreen's poverty had bred for it. Bad times had often made Tom talk of crossing 'the water'. And, domestically, times between Tom and herself had never been so bad as they were at that very day. Could Tom have gone off ... but no, she dismissed the idea. Nevertheless dark thoughts would not leave her as she circled the charabanc. One or two had indulged in too much sun or drink or both and sprawled inside already snoring. Kate intended to stay outside until Tom appeared and they could enter together as though nothing had happened.

From her vantage point Kate counted the people inside and could see the Tullyreen neighbours had all safely boarded the bus long before the appointed hour. Whatever glories or temptations Belfast and the Twelfth offered, the country folk took no chances of missing their only means of transport home. The driver was a stranger. They did not trust strangers on such occasions. Despair dropped Kate into a black hole of misery. Without Tom she could not go back to Tullyreen nor could she stay in Belfast, a city that had become more alien than if she had stood in Baghdad. And then she almost fainted when, without a word, Tom gently took her arm from behind and pushed her gently into the bus to take the only places that remained for them on the back seat. The long, exciting day had left the trippers so exhausted and anxious from home that they did not even ask Tom when 'the wee photos' would be ready. The neighbours shot sharp looks at them and Kate breathed with relief. They clearly thought she and Tom had been exploring Belfast together to the last possible minute.

The door slammed and the gears ground and the charabanc edged into the evening exodus. The other passengers watched how the driver, a stranger, was going to behave in all this traffic. Kate had eyes for nothing but Tom for had he got into the bus without his trousers she could not have been more amazed. No man in Tullyreen carried ferret box or shotgun over his shoulder with more pride than Tom wore his camera strap. Her silence was the measure of her sudden rise from despair to elation in having Tom once more beside her though bursting to ask where the camera had gone, for gone it certainly had.

Reproaches on its disappearance hovered on her lips but had he lost a hundred cameras Kate would not have cared. It had occurred to her already that the camera might not have been lost at all. Tom could have sold it to pay the bill of a knife-and-fork tea for the brazen girl pipers, though it would surprise Kate to hear he had been talked into giving it to the one who had laughingly claimed and got his buttonhole. The bus cleared the last straggling outskirts of Belfast before Tom spoke. Sweet air from the heavy green countryside rushed in the windows and mingled with the hot air inside which already reeked of orange peel and spilt stout. Tom's jacket lay on his knees and from its pocket he produced a small tin. 'I thought it about time we got that,' he said handing it to Kate. It was a tiny pot of black enamel paint.

For seven months they had talked of buying such a tin. The new bicycle had arrived with a scratch providing Tom with the kind of touching-up job he loved. But every time Kate went into town, the paint went out of her head. Now it lay slowly warming in her clammy hand. It produced mixed feelings—gratitude, and that on such a day he had remembered such an errand made the gratitude warmer than a tin of paint might normally earn, but with the gratitude went a special kind of Kate Lyttle feeling that the tiny tin was something of a booby prize if it was all that remained from the proceeds of his valuable camera. Still she refrained from questioning him, gauging his sheepish manner to be a confession not only of shame for his behaviour with the girl pipers, but also for his foolishness in parting with the camera in the heat of flirtation.

The charabanc reached Omagh before Kate judged it opportune to make the opening bid 'Lost your Kodak, then.' It came out more a statement than a question, betraying her note of surprise as false.

Omagh's lights disappeared behind them in the long summer twilight before Tom answered, and the delay confirmed the worst of Kate's speculations about him being a fool with the pipers. Eventually he volunteered, low so the neighbours would not hear, 'Don't you think we've had enough of cameras?'

Kate glanced involuntarily at the supply of cheap film on the luggage rack above them. However irritating his hours of developing in the scullery might be, she never forgot her mother's frequent comment that Tom's hobby made less demand on their budget than the neighbour's men's with their drinking and smoking and those in the terrace who had more racing pigeons than laying fowl.

'Old still waters,' Kate thought affectionately, glancing sideways at her husband who now joined the others rocked to sleep by the heat and motion. Where had he been all those hours? Not only that, but, and this worried her more, who had he been with? The hills around Tullyreen loomed in the distance as grey dove breasts nestling softly against buttermilk streaks of light under appearing stars. 'Curiosity isn't going to kill this cat,' Kate said to herself. She smiled. Cat was certainly the word. But never again. Cameras or no cameras, she swore never to nag Tom again. Her lonely panic-stricken hours in Belfast had been a warning. She had tasted widowhood. Until God took one of them, Kate would keep her wedding vows to love and to cherish. If Tom chose to tell her where he had been then she would listen. But if not, then she would not try to prise the oyster open, tonight or any other night. She wanted nothing more than to forget the whole outing. Wild horses would not drag her to Belfast again. But, although she did not know it then, far from forgetting the Twelfth of July in Belfast she would remember it all her life.

Next morning Tom got up earlier than usual and as Kate followed him down and busied herself at the fire she could hear him messing about in the turf shed. 'To keep out of my way,' she whispered to the ginger tom on the window sill. She packed Tom's midday piece and he left for his day's work at the creamery. He was whistling happily. Not until Kate went into the turf shed later did she find out why he went off whistling. All the previous day's mysteries were solved at once for there, already fixed on the Rudge, was a brand new chromium-plated dynamo set—lamp, wires, dynamo and all. Kate burst into tears and could not take hold of herself at all.

Cage

FOR NEARLY A YEAR NOW MAUREEN had been allowed to take Roy out by herself. With the dog loping along circumspectly at the end of the lead, she left the houses and the mill behind and walked as far as the beach stretched along the bay. But none of the other days when they had come to the beach were quite the same as this one. Even Roy sensed the urgent way that Maureen flung herself over the stones. He did his best to bring back the pebbles she threw. Maureen had never wanted to be by the shore and its lapping waves so much as now, because this morning she had started school.

Maureen hated it from the moment she got inside the iron gate. In the hard echoing, brown corridors the school stank of decay and disinfectant. The teacher of the lower infant class had shown her at which desk to sit. It was too hard. By putting out her leg Maureen could feel the iron bracket that curled out with ugly lumps to hold up the top. The lid was greasy where generations of infants had smeared greasy hands. At the furthest edge was a hole with a white china inkwell in it, but no ink. In the other half of the desk, which was a two-seater, sat a boy who, before playtime, had told her his name. He also told her the name of the boy behind them who wet his seat and was caned before their very eyes. Maureen had heard nothing so terrible in her life before as the whistle that cane made, nor the short cry the boy gave each time it struck his fingers. She was mortally afraid. Would she wet her own seat, Maureen wondered, as she used to wet her bed?

A panic seized Maureen in which she lost all sense of time. She forgot that soon she would be running home again down the street for dinner, and that, as always, her mother would be there. The infants' department seemed like a cold, sweat-smelling coffin where she and the others in her class were sealed as good as dead. Hatred of the harsh room and fear of the cane made Maureen quite incapable of taking in the teacher's words. Desperately Maureen tried to remember the number and position of her coat-peg in the corridor. It was her only link with the outside world. Not until playtime did she even think of Roy. Then tears filled her eyes because she imagined that she would never see him again. She would never get away from the cruel red bricks, the asphalt and brown tiled walls.

The bell let loose a gigantic upheaval. All twelve classes rushed into the playground in a chaotic flood of bodies which knocked Maureen and swept her along. She never liked crowds. People in them became unreal. They changed as though they wore masks so you couldn't recognise them. And they didn't mind if they pushed you or trod on your toes with their clumsy grown-ups' shoes. Maureen once waited outside the mill for a girl who worked there. She thought it would be nice to walk home with her older friend. But a hooter had blasted and from the door hundreds of girls poured on to the pavement, girls who looked larger than usual and whose voices were louder and harsher than when they came into her mother's shop. And Maureen had not seen her friend. Cowering against the mill wall she waited until the last girls left and then she went home, too astonished to tell her mother.

School playtime was the same. The other children behaved quite differently from when they played in the street. Boys and girls Maureen knew quite well outside seemed disintegrated into fragments of fear and cruelty. None of them said or did things they would normally. School seemed to tear them, and when released from the classroom they turned to rend each other also. The boy in Maureen's desk tried to kiss her, not out of affection but from vindictiveness because he knew she would not like it. She ran into the girls' lavatory to escape him, but another girl held her in a cubicle by leaning against the door. Maureen screamed, for she hated confined places, but the older girl would not release her, until Maureen gave up her new red pencil in exchange for a pen with a glass barrel that showed the ink. Making her escape from the lavatory Maureen looked about the playground for seclusion. There seemed to be nothing but desperate groups of boys and girls imprisoned by railings and high walls. They were supposed to play in this dismal yard. But everyone behaved like wild beasts. The slightest weakness was seized on by a group of bullies as sport.

Maureen already knew Stewart Wilson. He was the biggest boy in the school. He came to her mother's shop quite often, and in spite of being much older he was shy and gentle with Maureen when he spoke to her. Stewart stuttered. Alone with Maureen's mother, chatting over the counter the stutter was hardly noticeable. With strangers, however, or when worried, Stewart became almost incomprehensible. Now Maureen could see him penned in a corner by a gang of seniors, goading and baiting him with the unpronounceable *st, st.* Shame filled Maureen to see her friend humiliated. She could do nothing to help him and went to hide herself under the iron fire escape. Six-sided holes studded the treads and Maureen stuck each of her fingers in to see if they would fit. Then she leaned back against one of the dustbins that lived under the fire escape.

Through her frock the ribbed metal made strange lines on her back. Her feet rested against a shiny iron pillar that held the stairs up. When the teacher on duty was not looking, the older boys slid down the pillars. Maureen had heard about this forbidden pastime even before she went to the school. Her neighbour Maggie Greer did it once and was caned six times for that, and another six for showing her drawers. None of the boys were doing it now. They were tormenting Stewart and calling him a jinny because of his funny way of talking. Stewart was no jinny to Maureen. She had often watched him sliding down the columns of the railway bridge, which were much longer than the fire escape ones. And he walked along the bridge parapet too, which nobody else dared to do.

Walking along the shore with Roy at the end of her first day listening to the noises of the waves, Maureen could only remember one other incident. Before the playtime finished some boys snatched her hair ribbon. She had not cried because of that but because they jeered at her for being the daughter of Bikson's bakery. For them this was worse than even Stewart Wilson's stutter. She belonged to a world envied by the ever-hungry and never-satisfied boys at the school. Maureen often saw them peering through the shop window, especially when the smell of fresh baking still hung in the air of the small street like the smell of incense and snuffed candles lingering in an empty chapel. And the boys resented Maureen because she represented the cause of their frustration. So often they wanted her mother's baking, but had no money. Bikson's was famous for streets around, and the fame was built on its wheaten and soda farls, and more especially on its potato-bread. The big well-done potato farls were eaten hot from the griddle by the message boys. On Friday nights the shop was stormed by mill-girls for the potato-apple. As the heiress to such a kingdom of pure delight Maureen was to be tormented. The boys hurt her most by scathing rhymes about her mother's perfect baking:

Bikson's taddy-bread
Lies on your belly like lead,
Give it a kick
And make it go quick,
Bikson's taddy-bread.

Roy came gasping from the water's edge with a stick of

driftwood in his mouth. Maureen tugged and the more she pulled, the harder Roy's teeth gripped. She wondered why he never tore the tender sides of his mouth which looked like a half-eaten kipper. The look in his eye was a mixture of wickedness, caution and love. He growled and pretended to be cross, but just enough to let her know he was not. And he only tugged lightly so that she would not let go. He kept glancing up at her, quick movements of his eye to see if Maureen understood. Next to her mother, Maureen loved Roy best in the world. He depended on her. He would let her do anything with him, even let her dress him up and put him in the pram. As she looked at those beseeching eyes Maureen remembered Roy's expression when she came home from school at dinner-time. A cold nose had come against her legs and did not leave them until she went back in the afternoon. Roy had never known her to be so long away from home before. He also understood that something had brought her unhappiness.

When she ducked under the counter and burst into the kitchen, Maureen had been scarcely able to believe that home was still intact. Isolation in the school made her think that somehow everything would be changed when she finally escaped. But her mother was there, the same as always, mashing potatoes with a big wooden beetle. Tears of terror changed to tears of relief but Maureen kept them back. Her mother would be upset and besides, they never made a noise in the kitchen. For as long as she could remember, any commotion down below had brought a cannonade of knocking from the floor above—Great-Aunt Mary Ann Bikson, the invalid. It was her name which had been painted on the shop nameboard. Now the paint was faded and flaking, like great-aunt herself. She lived entirely in an armchair. Maureen was a little afraid of her and on account of this could not love her as much as she loved Roy. Yet she thought the old lady wonderful for refusing to budge from the armchair day or night. Mary Ann had it firmly fixed in her shrivelled head that if she got into her bed she would die. Maureen once persuaded her mother to let her sleep in an armchair. The excitement wore off after about half an hour and it was so uncomfortable that Maureen crept up to her own bed. After that, Great-Aunt Mary Ann always seemed odd to her and Maureen was not out of sympathy with the street-boys who sometimes opened the letterbox and shouted through

Our wee Mary Ann's
The devil for a man.

Maureen had gone to the old lady's room specially to tell her great-aunt that she would be starting school on the Monday and the old lady appeared to understand. But at four o'clock when Maureen went up to pour out the day's doings and about the alphabet and the plasticine, Mary Ann had merely remarked rather sharply that Maureen's ribbon was creased and askew. Maureen thought this a silly thing to say. The old lady ought to have realised that there were boys in the school, the same boys who shouted through the letterbox and called her an 'old besom'. Maureen did not linger with her great-aunt but ran downstairs, put Roy on his lead and hurried to the sea.

And that was how she came to be walking once more along the shore, but this time saddened with the knowledge of good and evil. The first day at school had taught her nothing except how much she belonged to the beach, and how she could be happy there alone with Roy.

Until they were free of all the buildings Roy had to be kept on his lead. He waited patiently for he knew that as soon as they came within sight and smell of the sea he would be free. Maureen always hurried over the first part of their journey. She stepped precisely between the joints of the paving slabs, sometimes doing a kind of hopscotch step. The linen mill was almost the last building before the beach, and here Maureen ran. The mill's weird smell, not quite of currants nor of new paint, reminded her too much of the day when she had been caught in the rush of mill girls. Free of the mill, Maureen and Roy passed between the three bollards in Doland's Entry, and raced over the bridge at the far end. They had to make sure of getting over the bridge while no train was passing underneath. To be on it as the structure shook to the thunder of train wheels would bring bad luck. Beyond the rank nettles on one side of the road lay the stonemason's yard where Sandy sat chipping away at little girl angels and stone Bibles. All the angels had identical faces and identical bunches of marble violets and all the Bibles lay open at the same page. She didn't mind the whiteness and deadness of it all because Sandy winked at her and called to Roy if he saw them, although Maureen was glad he never stopped them for she would not have known what to say to a man who made angels.

Roy and she did not pause at all until they got to the old iron bedstead leading into Johnston's horse field. And Maureen had to stop there, for her mother allowed her no further. She could easily get to the beach from there, although here again she must not wander too far. Maureen never went on to the beach straightaway. She liked to savour the place, smell its tingling air like a connoisseur with his nose in a glass of Malmsey. By climbing on the bars of the bedstead Maureen experienced the climax of their walk. The sea sprang into view over the rocks. It was a wide sea hardly showing at all because it lay so flat under the sky. On some days the sea disappeared in mists or merged into low cloud. On other days the sea was as dark as ink, flecked with white stripes where the wind was blowing up high foam-crested waves. But the sea was the most beautiful in summer when sparkling over its whole surface, as though sprinkled with diamonds. Before reaching the lane's end Maureen could tell whether it was rough on the shore, for the winds carried long tongues of seaweed and tied them to the bedstead where they fluttered like her mother's silk stockings. Maureen was only allowed to venture on to the beach itself during fine and calm weather. On rough days she clung precariously to the bedstead and kept an eye on Roy as he ran in and out among the rocks and pebbles. She sat as long as possible watching the endless waves breaking on the black, sandy bay. She wondered where all the waves came from and why they made up their minds to come in at *her* particular part of the shore.

The sea sounds and the trills of oyster-catchers and the whistling of the wind bemused the little girl sitting on the bedstead. By the sea she was transformed. To be on the shore with Roy was like a beautiful dream, which nevertheless was more real than her ordinary life at home or school. And the waves not only made music but brought smells of the sea and even these were more exciting than the smell of the best golden maize farls being baked at home. The winds also played with her copper hair stroking it on calm days but tossing it on wild ones.

Dulse was blown up to the iron bedstead and she could pick this off and eat it. Because it came from the sea she loved, Maureen thought the salty, anchovy-tasting seaweed far better to eat than Bangor rock or acid drops. It made a sort of communion with the fishes and elusive mermaids and dark forests of seaweed that waved on the seabed. But Maureen did not like the carrageen moss which she also collected, for it seemed so much part of Great-Aunt Mary Ann who lived almost entirely on jellies made from it.

An instinct told Maureen when half-past five came round. Standing on the rails again for a last view of the sea and the blue hills on the farther side of the bay, she called Roy and started home again. Whatever he might be doing Roy always followed at her summons. They had to cross the bridge again before the five-thirty charged by and the mill girls exploded out of their grey prison.

Maureen's life gradually became like the unchanging rhythms of the tides and the winds and the seasons. School became bearable though not likeable and almost a necessary opposite to the shore's wild freedom. Soon after she left the infants for the juniors and went into school by a different gate, Roy died. Maureen's heart broke at the sight of her friend lying so still in his basket. She had not even said a special goodbye to him before going to bed, not thinking that he would die in the night. Even though her mother explained that all living things die as surely as they are born, Maureen could find no consolation. With tears she went to the bedstead leading into the horse field and listened to the wind. And when she got home a new puppy was flopping about on the floor, and she could not help but love it. The puppy became part of her life, just like the raffia work and the recitation periods in school which were the two things that least irritated her. At times, geography with Miss Glenmann who had been to China was passable for she talked about the sea and the distant countries it connected with their own part of the Ulster shore.

Two years after the first day at school Maureen began swimming lessons with other eight-year-old children. Her performance was good and though the swimming instructor's praise encouraged her, Maureen's mind was fixed on an ambition quite other than learning to swim well. Scripture lessons in the infants had been given from large pictures hung over the blackboard and unrolled to show the temples of Egypt or the Red Sea dividing, Job's boils or Elijah going up to heaven with his grand pony and trap, and the shores of Galilee and the fishermen throwing their nets. And of course Jesus doing all sorts of impossible but exciting things like making dead people not dead and also walking on the sea. Maureen could never see enough of the picture which showed Jesus standing on the water and smiling in an amused way at poor Peter who was floundering only a few feet away. Maureen had no sympathy with the tiresome disciple at all, and nothing but admiration for Jesus. After all, Peter was such a simpleton. All you needed was enough faith and the trick was done. And it was Maureen's great aim in life now to walk on the sea, with the new dog beside her. It would be wonderful just to step off the rocks and go out on the waves like a seagull, only walking instead of sitting.

The only difficulty Maureen encountered was how to know whether she had got enough faith to try the experiment. She imagined it to be some kind of banking process where good deeds were put in a credit account and when it amounted to the equivalent of a fortune then the sea-walking could begin. Her progress with the swimming lessons showed good buoyancy which indicated that her faith account must be full. It ought to be, for Maureen always took care to be good. Once she found a sixpence on her way to the beach and she had been happy to put half of it in the mission box for the leper babies of Africa. And never once since deciding to be good had she looked at either Roy or the new dog doing their little business on the waste ground. All at once one afternoon during a tiresome arithmetic lesson, Maureen decided to try her faith that evening. Being a Wednesday her mother would close the shop at dinner-time and come with her. To have her mother witness the miracle of faith would crown Maureen's joy.

No longer could she bear not to be able to walk along the waves' crests or along the golden wake of the setting sun. Maureen went with her mother to the beach and, without stopping by the iron bedstead, scrambled over the rocks to a large, black sewer pipe. It looped across the beach like a black sea monster and plunged into the water some yards from the shore. Knowing that Maureen could swim and often played by the water's edge her mother felt no alarm at the way her young daughter walked down the pipe in such a determined way. She glanced up from her knitting just in time to see Maureen hauling herself out of the water looking cross and bedraggled. For three weeks after the failure of her miracle Maureen did not say her prayers, she was so disillusioned in her Maker.

After the initial disillusionment Maureen carefully examined the situation and came to the conclusion that it had not been God's fault but her own. By putting on her swimming costume before walking on the sewer she had doubted. There could hardly be a greater sign of her lack of faith. In the sea-walking picture Jesus had worn His long blue dress, yet she had feared to spoil her new frock and so Maureen knew that she had not believed enough.

Maureen was glad that she could blame herself and not the sea for her failure. To the running waves and the rocks she felt no antagonism and soon forgot the incident altogether in the wider freedom acquired by growing older. Maureen scarcely stopped to wonder at her love of the long curving bay and the scimitar sweep of it right round to the headland which dropped sheer into the crashing breakers at its foot. Farmers threw their dead animals over this point and a herring boat had been wrecked there. As the bay swept away from the town it became lonelier. Sheds and wooden shacks, once used for now forgotten purposes, struggled for a short distance beyond the town. Then they too stopped and after them Maureen was quite alone with the dog and the gulls that wheeled up screaming at their approach. As she progressed, each secret pool between the rocks, each round pebble seemed more marvellous than the last. Maureen beachcombed the long forlorn side of the bay where neither children could paddle during the day nor tinker find shelter enough at night. Cast up by the tides were lines of seaweed and wrack which followed the shore as though the rails of a vanished railway had once run there. Maureen followed these tide marks keeping her eyes on the beach, her gutties wet from kicking the seaweed over. Maureen had no desire for cast-up treasures, rings or gold trinkets, but only for small pieces of glass or oddly-coloured stones exquisitely and finely ground and polished by the vast movements of storms and tides. The best of these, worthless, precious objects were placed on her window sill or locked in the old trunk under the stairs. None of her *objets trouvés* served any special purpose, except the salty dulse and Great-Aunt's carrageen moss, and smooth bones of cuttlefish. The soft white bone could be rubbed on her mother's grater to make wonderful tooth powder.

Not until her twelfth birthday did Maureen take the dog and go at night to the far side of the bay. The sun went down behind the headland and night winds crept about the sea and the shore blowing from nowhere and from everywhere. No children came at that time of the day to make rocks ring with shrieks. Apart from the wind and the gulls' infrequent night cries there was no sound except from the boatyard. Gleams from the lamps streamed out of the open door, peculiarly yellow in the indigo darkness. Waves caught the light and broke it in fragments, throwing the glistening patches about. Maureen could stand by the low wooden slipway admiring the proud forms of a new boat taking shape in the shed. Building a boat became a greater miracle for Maureen than walking on the sea had once seemed. She had watched this boat emerge from timber stacked in the yard. The men worked the wood shaping it with saw, chisel and hammer, making the bones and covering them with the shapely flesh of planking. Soon it would be finished, bright as a gull with paint. Then, quite simply, it would go down the slipway and ride the sea, light, buoyant, its bows turned to the horizon. Maureen wished she could help. A boat was a better thing to make than the school raffia table-mats, better too than the stools and pipe-racks the boys made at their woodwork class.

Inside the shed, his face ruddy in the hurricane lamp's gentle light, was Stewart Wilson. Since leaving school he had grown suddenly into a young man. Boyish roundness had gone from his face, and the firmness of a man's was already nascent. He smoked a pipe and was serious. Unlike her mother's shop or the mill, the boatyard did not keep to regular hours of work, stopping at six o'clock. The men's life belonged to the boat and they could not rest until it breasted the waves. Stewart did not see the little girl who stood in the shadow by the door watching him pass the plane over the planks. He did not notice that her bright eyes followed every curl of wood that rose with the faintest sigh and fell like a yellow autumn leaf to the floor. Stewart and the other two men he worked with would have eyes for nothing until their boat was running in and out, and loading its herring on the quay before even school started in the mornings. Maureen lingered at the boatshed on those nights when high tide cut off the farther side of the bay, the empty shore from which she could look back at the twinkling town, the golden lights of the streets and the stardust of the little harbour and the waterside sheds, all so warm under the icy stars

Nothing disturbed the placid beauty of Maureen's life. No dramatic events were needed to give excitement, nor tragedies to give it poignancy. Every gale that thundered up from the sea which tore it to shreds, every languishing summer twilight that gave the day a second youth, every breeze that trailed cirrus feathers across the sky as though a celestial seagull hung poised in the staring blue, all these filled Maureen's life with more emotion than she could bear. The promise of adolescence began to colour her thoughts just as the horizon was tinted before the sun came up.

Whenever the weather was good enough Maureen took her much-resented school homework and sat with it on the old iron bedstead. The sea beat time at her feet and she passed her tongue over her lips as she did when writing, the taste of salt was on them. On one particular late afternoon she just could not get the four standard verses to rhyme in spite of having brought the Church Hymnal for reference. The work aggravated Maureen for it was the only flaw in an otherwise perfect hour. Earlier in the day the sea had been agitated but now it had subsided and lay calm, turning little waves quietly and gently along the whole sweep of the bay. The waders too were still, the absence of their liquid trills was uncanny. Maguire's geese farther up the lane made landlubber noises as they plundered a mangel-pit. Maureen could not concentrate on the tedious poetry exercise, for the gilded afternoon loosed a flow of images in her mind that would not be suppressed.

Over an old quarry behind her a bird wheeled in suspended flight. Maureen followed each pivot turn of slim body on taut wings. The movements were sparse and strong, as though the bird had concern for nothing except the serried buttresses of rock below, the black spectrum flash in space of its own body, the wheel, droop and turn of pregnant days by the sea. A desire for wings seized Maureen. She wanted to mount air and soar over the highest flower on the quarry's terrible, grass-forelocked precipice and then sweep down to the shanny-pools where an old bicycle wheel lay half-drowned, with its spokes curled like fingers trying to be tongues. Yet at the same time Maureen was content in being earthbound. She belonged no less to the wildlife of the shore which was hers as the chasm quarry was the bird's. Her wanderings and lingerings were shore-life as much as the bird dropping like a bolt or up-breasting on any breath of wind that escaped to the coast.

When Maureen jumped down from the bedstead and picked her way across rock pools to the bay's farther side, she saw her reverie had been spied on by two girls from her class. They jeered and called her an eejit because on passing Maureen had not noticed them. Even when they shouted she ignored them being so rapt in the bird over the quarry. But the girls were merciless and spread it around the school that Maureen was wrong in the head. At first the other children mocked her and then began to whisper and give her sidelong glances. But none of this worried Maureen overmuch. Not from the day she had rested for the first time against the fire escape had she ever been popular, and Maureen would not force her company where it was not wanted. She ignored the girls' teasings and felt it little loss that the boys wrote her no notes. She could hardly wait now until her last day at school, the day when she would walk through the gates and never return.

When free Maureen would devote herself wholly to the shop. Now that Great-Aunt Mary Ann was dead and lying under one of Sandy's stone Bibles, the shop would one day be Maureen's to continue the tradition of high-class baking in the third generation. Maureen wanted nothing other than what the small square-windowed house and the tiny shop could give her. Talk of a career away in Derry or other strange cities concerned her not at all. Life for her meant filling a small gap in the town and being near the sea. She envied nobody and coveted nothing.

Summer and winter, night and day she went to the beach as before, though the puppy which had replaced Roy was now an old dog himself. At seventeen Maureen had grown tall and shapely. The copper hair had darkened and its sheen was like the moon on the sea. Her eyes were wide and showed her to be lost in dreams of no substance. Maureen scarcely recalled how, as a child, she had feared the linen mills, its crowds and sickening smell and how carefully she had avoided the railway bridge if a train was due. She forgot how large the iron bedstead had seemed to her in those days. It was rusty now and half-buried by the strangling embrace of devil's garter.

Maureen was no longer afraid to go right into the boatyard and talk to the men as they worked, for now she brought them bread when they were too busy to come and collect it themselves. Without realising what had happened both Maureen and the boatbuilders had come to anticipate her visits. Pausing for a moment from work, Stewart Wilson would wipe sweat from his brow and glance towards the open doors and the sea beyond. He would take a deep breath and scan the horizon, as though looking for signs of a weather change, or sight of a fishing boat slipping out of the harbour. But he was hoping that a young girl's figure would suddenly appear in the opening. Sometimes he was lucky, and Maureen would step quietly over the wood, perhaps bring a porringer of willucks to share with him. For Maureen, her visits to the boatshed were full of a magic she failed to understand. A feeling possessed her that she belonged there even more than to her mother's shop. In the boatshed a glow of wellbeing filled Maureen, a sweet, deep contentment. Not only the men working there responded kindly to her but even the wood and the tools, the long-line baskets and old eel rakes seemed like living creatures who waited and welcomed her.

She did not think of Stewart as being part of the boatyard, but rather as the other men and the work on the boats as being the ambience which mysteriously surrounded Stewart. But Maureen was not conscious of this. If friends had teased her about Stewart she would have laughed, believing her denial of interest in him to be the truth. But she went to the shed several times a day and a conviction grew in her that the resin and tar smelling yard held the essence of her life along the shore. It became her small universe.

Maureen thought that the old boatbuilder fascinated her because he showed her many fishermen's tricks, such as how to make a feather lure for catching pollack, or a horsehair frog for the codlings. The old man's tough brown hand dusted with wood ash and rolling horsehairs against an iron thigh was manhood for Maureen. The boatbuilder's hands were the sort a man should have, not the flabby hands which youths from the model school had. Yet her real reason for admiring those work-hardened hands was because they were like Stewart's. Or at least, Stewart's hands would be like that when maturity weathered him. At that time Maureen confused Stewart and the other men in a general impression of manliness. It remained for Stewart himself to awaken true sight in her eyes.

Still unchanged was the lure of the bay's remote side. All Maureen's longings and dreams belonged to the untouched shore where the driftwood went uncollected and the redshanks undisturbed. Maureen's delight in beachcombing was the same, a smoothed piece of bottle was still for her more precious than anything in the jeweller's window in the town. At night she still tried to read meaning into the winking lights beyond the bay. And her eighteenth birthday had gone before she found the meaning, and the power that pushes the seas and makes the sun shine and the moon to give light by night, and the stars in the firmament to be so fiery.

A new boat had been launched from the yard in fine style. Maureen and her mother made a sight of scones and fancies for the celebration. To get everything ready in time they both got up at three in the morning, and that Maureen was sleepy long before the old boatbuilder took his melodeon and the lads their partners, was not surprising. When the dancing began Maureen collected the empty plates and stole out of the boatyard unnoticed, or so she thought. A soft voice behind her asked, 'Aren't ya goin' to give us 'Turkey in the Straw'?'

Stewart was beside her, burning her with the slow fire of his smile. He took the basket and walked along with her. He did not talk much but when he did Maureen noticed he no longer stuttered. He walked close to her so that they felt the movement in each other's bodies. The wind was freshening and Maureen suddenly knew that she wanted Stewart to shield her, that she wanted him to be with her always by the bay and along the beach. He spoke quietly of the boat they had just finished and how he had done more towards it than any other boat since he had worked in the yard. Maureen was not listening to what he said but only to the throaty music of his voice, the stillness and warmth in it. He was so close she could smell the tarry, sawdust smell of the yard on his thick seaman's jersey. Lightly she touched his brown, bare forearm.

By the iron bedstead leading into Johnston's horse-field they sat down and looked towards the town lights. Maureen had never known such sweetness.

'It's a fine night,' said Stewart, again in that soft lilting voice.

'There'll be rain before mornin', though,' replied Maureen watching clouds that skimmed the remains of a moon.

'Ya can see they've put the Tilley lamp in Brown's parlour,' added the boy. He gently turned Maureen's head so that she could see the harsher light amongst the cascade of lighted windows that tumbled down the hill along the quay.

'They say we'll have electric down the yard by next spring.'

Stewart took Maureen's hand and she was surprised to feel how hot they were, and how tenderly they could hold hers in spite of being so strong and hard. Maureen wondered why it had not occurred to her before that the bay was more beautiful with a boy beside her. But perhaps she had thought so and dismissed the idea. She could not take just anybody to her bay and show him its secrets. Stewart understood. He built boats because he understood.

'What's the light beyond Montgomery's old kelp kiln?' she asked him aloud.

Together they tried to piece the fragments of light together, fitting houses and streets together to make up the picture so familiar by day. Maureen knew the houses but Stewart knew the jetties and the stretches of quay and who owned the boats and creel-sheds.

Peering into the darkness, measuring now the nearness of the houses, now the remoteness of the stars, now the undetermined distance of fishing boat lights on the sea, Maureen grew

conscious of a cage which surrounded Stewart and herself. The
cage-bars were invisible, but defined. An ecstasy ran through her
body as Stewart leaned closer. What a little cage they lived in,
but what infinities it enclosed. With sweetness flowing through
her, Maureen knew that she and Stewart would be joined
together like two waves running and merging into one. Their
whole lives would be spent along the few miles of shore where
moon-varnished tides ebbed so low revealing the old stone
fishing weirs.

Then she remembered her earlier experience when she
watched the black bird planing in great curves over the quarry,
as though the quarry was a cage and the wide sky could not be
reached. She thought then that each turn and dive of the bird's
stiff wings drew an invisible line, constructing a cage of loci
beyond which it could not fly. When she had wanted to borrow
its wings to give her heart the means to soar, she had thought, 'I
will fly up until I am no more than a cleg in the sky and then
turn to the islands and fly over oceans and continents, blown by
the wind to the world's end.' The bird's skimming the quarry
walls had seemed then an imprisonment. Now she understood.

She had never regarded herself as prisoner to the confines of
town and shore. From the moment when she took Roy for a walk
after her first day at school, Maureen had known freedom. Once
past the railway bridge and along as far as the bedstead by
Johnston's horse-field Maureen found boundless skies and seas,
and endless wonder in the smallest pool, a magnitude of
grandeur in the tiniest rocks. With the years coming and going
along the shore every day, with the up and out on the rocks, with
the down and back of her leaping from bursting bladderwrack to
crunching sword razor, Maureen knew now that she had been
weaving her own locus cage. It was as big as the universe, and as
small as a particle of wind-blown spray.

And with an inner eye she saw the bird's movements over the
quarry again, and the wings were not weaving confining bars but
bars to protect and secure. And as she had compassed the bird's
movements in a glance, so now Maureen had compassed her

whole life. Stewart would be beside her, as he was now, in the years that lay ahead, years that stretched into the future like the rocks and pools stretched round a perspective of the bay. Maureen would be in perpetual bliss, the bliss of insignificant things. She had woven her cage as a spider spins its web and it sparkled blissfully now almost visibly like a dew-hung web.

A Fine Lady

THE MCFINNS WERE LEVEL-CROSSING FOLK, and their railway dwelling was of the tiniest. And, to Eileen's mind at least, no cottage for miles had more grandeur or finer spring wells, what with their big close of Aran Banners and turf stack to hold out the longest winter. Eileen was seven and already allowed to take the goats as far as the second plantation to tether them. Besides their two closes the McFinns had the grazing along two or three lush miles of railway verges, from the level-crossing gates right up to the blacksmith's forge. Eileen grew up alongside the bright, shiny steel track. It had always been there, like a river running curiously straight into a far country. The possibility that there was a time, once, when there had been no railway, never entered her head. Certain things had a fixed, eternal existence. The sun was one, the railway was another.

Yet Eileen was aware of transcience. Seven, she knew, was different from being five years of age. And like the railway line running immeasurably ahead, Eileen realised that she would grow even older, eventually becoming a woman like her mother. In a way, she could see all this happening with the goats, except that they grew up quicker than people. In her seven-year span she had already seen one or two of the older ones die. That was how living things were different from the sun or the railway which had always been there and always would be.

Transcience. Eileen's strong instinct for preservation imbued her with the sense of superstition which governed the older people's lives. When reduced to essentials, there were few effective means which people could use to protect their vulnerable lives. Nothing could ever harm the sun, and the railway was reparable when it went wrong. The men brought their picks to sing on the stones outside and set their black billies to sing over their fires. Nothing could happen to the railway line. But people were different. They could be killed, like the cattle-drover at the level-crossing, or they could be ill. Many of them loosened their grip on ordinary things and had to be put away in Omagh. Others gave up trying and became the tramps whom she found curled up asleep near the railway verges.

Yet a simple enough ritual existed to forestall misfortune. The coal, for instance, was one way. If you picked up a lump fallen from a passing train, spat on it and then threw it over your left shoulder, this was a sound bringer of good luck. Trailing the goats on their various ropes, Eileen kept close to the track because she wanted the coal. Only she did not throw the pieces over her shoulder with much force because she had to collect them and take them home afterwards. They gave such heavenly heart to the turves on the fire. If Eileen threw the lumps too hard, they shattered and the fragments were difficult to gather.

Everybody Eileen knew did this to coal; her parents, brothers, sisters and even Uncle Reuben down in the forge who, quite plainly, had no need of good luck and was therefore like the sun. He had never been ill, he was unlikely ever to die in spite of great age, and he had a mint of money. It was all said to be stowed away in the big jars which once had been used for the pickling of cows' heads. And Eileen knew there were many of the jars, for her great-uncle remembered seeing at one time eighty cows' and pigs' heads pickled and standing on the kitchen shelves. But that had been in the old days, when her great-grandfather was a renowned spade-maker, making the slanes to measure. Because he was the smith he had received his rightful portion of every beast that was killed in the townland—in his case it was always the heads. Eileen liked to hear of the old man, for she possessed an oatcake toaster he had made out of old horseshoes.

Yet in spite of the fame and reputation of the forge, Uncle Reuben was the biggest family joke on account of the moleskin coat and trousers which he still wore, being the ones he married in fifty and more years before. But, invincible though he was, Uncle Reuben always spat on any lump of coal he found in his path. And since Eileen was too young to question the efficacy of this habit, it took her quite a long time each morning to go along the verges to the goats' tethering place.

More than anyone else in her family, Eileen considered, she wanted good luck. Hers was a desperate, urgent need. More than once as she sat on the sheltered, sun-warm verges, she had dreamed of the day when she would have silks to cover her bed and a clean shift twice a week. This plan for the future in no way intruded on the present to make discontentment. About her present existence Eileen wanted no change. Her dreams of one day being a lady and having water in a tap like castle folk, did not make her any less willing now to be useful about the house. At any time her mother might ask, Eileen would do her own special little dance-run, hopping from sleeper to sleeper for the whole two miles down to the forge. This might be to get a porringer of water from the forge cooling trough so that her mother might mix it with tormenting roots for rumbles in man or beast. But as she went in her odd jumps along the track her thoughts would be on big dresses and dainty china plates— though this notion of gentility did not stop her from trying to get the biggest spoon in the dresser when her mother set the pot of stirabout on a stool and they all dug into it together.

Seven years of age is quite old. Besides ambition, love and hate are formed, not only as potentials but as actual experience towards real people. Eileen could reckon on her dad's special interest in her. He had enough children to afford the luxury of favouritism without depriving the rest of affection. There were so many that nobody seemed to notice that he doted on one particularly. Eileen, for her part, received this affection warily and gratefully. There certainly could be no question of taking advantage from it. At the lowest level, it meant that Eileen was the only one not afraid of her father when he came home drunk from the fair. On these occasions she had no difficulty in being allowed to stay up late to cook his boxty supper.

Big Sandy was never so drunk as he liked to pretend. As soon as he and Eileen were alone he quietened down, took her on his knee and made her feel in his pocket for the big bag of rhubarb rock which after fair day was always there. Then he had to put each piece of rock into her tiny hands. He loved the hot, expectant little palms which were perfectly complementary to his own granite-like fists. One by one, Big Sandy touched Eileen's fingers as though unable to believe their frailty was real.

Eileen learnt a host of jingles from her father. His memory for such things was prodigious. Her favourite was:

Lisnaskea for drinking tea
Maguiresbridge for brandy,
Lisbellaw for wapping straw
Enniskillen the dandy.

With such rhymes in her head going on and on like the ringing of changes, Eileen would let herself be chased up to bed in the loft. On the evenings when her father got out his Orange sash from the biscuit tin on top of the dresser, she went to bed later than any other night. She waited up by the fire until Big Sandy came in from the Lodge meeting and put the sash with its silver fringe away. It lived in the tin with the war medals and the family birth certificates—like a sacred guard against the Fenian men up at the chapel crossroads. Eileen sat silent but wide-eyed as her father, with just a hint of teasing, warmed her the sweetest of red-biddy.

He winked broadly at his little girl, and raising their mugs they gave the toast to 'The Pope and the pillory with the Devil pelting priests at him'. Lodge nights were the nights of the year—better by far than the big fair at Derrygonnelly or the coming of the Straw Boys at Christmas. With the last drop of hot wine drained Eileen went off to bed already in a dream.

But she could not sleep straightaway but waited instead for her father's last noises downstairs. However sore his poor head might be after the drinking, he never once forgot to take a bit of food out to his terrier bitch, and however tight his boots might be, he never loosened the leather laces until he had set a dish of milksops on the hearth for the crickets which lived in the cracks behind the open fire.

After jaunts to the fair or the Lodge-room Big Sandy never cared to trust his limbs on the rickety staircase to the loft. Eileen wondered why he preferred to sprawl uncomfortably on the settle in front of the fire. He ought to have gone up to the warm loft by the chimney-stack where all the rest of them slept together in the best of feather ticks. Although Eileen was full of human understanding and could read people's moods like Archer the shepherd read the sky, she did not fully appreciate the effects of alcohol in her father combined with those of religious conversion in her mother.

Here was a situation too complex for a child to understand. Somehow, somewhen, Big Sandy and his wife had come to a point where physical contact between them was distasteful, and, as usual in such circumstances, within themselves they both blamed the other. There could never be any tracing back now to the original withdrawal, the first coldness. Perhaps she resented him for having worn her out with so many children, or perhaps he objected to the deep weariness in the body which had once been so pliant in his rocky hands.

Sandy, of course, had always been a drinker, but after the coldness he began to drink more. Eileen's mother had grounds then for real complaint. But instead of nagging him she went and got herself 'saved' at the very next tent meeting and did her hair in a Pilgrim bun. And being 'saved', she considered that she should not do in the bed all sorts of things that even at this late

stage Big Sandy thought she should. Consequently, because his
wife was 'saved', Sandy compensated himself by even wilder
drinking. And so the cycle began again. It was a chain with no
weak links. Eileen's mother was more than content to lay her
down each night in the strong, if invisible, arms of her Saviour.
The smell of the night through the skylight and the back-scratch
from little Jimmy the nestlecock sufficed her through the dark
hours. As for Big Sandy, he grew accustomed to a celibate,
drunken state and he felt his manhood not entirely wasted as
long as he could gaze on its sweet fruit, the blue-eyed Eileen.

Eileen never knew exactly when she fell asleep.
Unconsciously, she waited for her father to come upstairs,
though she understood he never would. Snug though the loft
might be and loud the crickets' song, Eileen was always happy
when her bantam cock heralded a new day and she could be up
and downstairs to close the level-crossing gate for the first train.
When it came and the driver waved to her from the cab and she
had opened the gates again, Eileen was away down the verges
with the goats.

Eileen was not at all impressed by her mother's religion. It
could not compare with her father's free and easy ways. There
were moments, especially during the wildest storms at night with
the dread fear of the archangels blowing their trumpets to take her
mother and the Pilgrims all away to heaven at the Last Day, when
Eileen was terrified. Yet strangely, her mother was equally taken
up with the fact that she was the third generation of celebrated
bunion charmers. She would also slip one of her lucky threepenny
bits in the churn, in order to hasten the butter. And all the
Pilgrims hymns would be forgotten before the milk turned, for her
mother would be chanting old pagan verses to the churnstaff:

> *Rise butter rise, my dash grown light,*
> *And not a tinker's skite of loss*
> *When halse and holly bear thy cross,*
> *Rise butter rise, my dash grow light.*

But Eileen was as sure of her father's esteem as she was of the sun's unfailing daily run. Big Sandy took none of his children with him on his poaching excursions except Eileen. Sandy did not wait for the quality and their water-bailiffs to come trolling with golden sprat for the spring salmon. When the grilse arrived with bluebells and red clover down by the banks on the castle shore, Sandy was not thinking of winning his turf. And there was always brown trout or ferox when the lordly gillaroo made itself scarce in the shallows. Eileen loved her dad at all times, but she worshipped him when the both of them were away through the plantation and Graham's meadows to the silent waters of the pre-dawn. Pheasant broth which her mother served up when she came back from school always tasted better if she had been out in the twilight kill.

By her eighth birthday Eileen could tell well enough when there were snipe in the bottoms by the river and which of the rabbit runs was good for a snare. Fine big hands though her brothers might possess, Eileen was never in doubt that it would be herself whom Big Sandy would ask to go ferreting in the hills when all else failed to grace the Sabbath table. God was good to her father, Eileen thought many times as she followed him home down the hill where he went with a woodcock hanging from each pocket of his old army jacket or the char swinging on a sally rod.

This life, the round, the pattern of her days was never upset by Eileen's dreams of becoming a fine lady. Being so young, she did not think that she would have to change, and that the level-crossing life would vanish. She imagined that a wand would be waved and, abracadabra, there she would be, in all her finery. Since her idea of future grandeur was never confided to anyone there was nobody to point out to her that she would be unable to have both the old, railway life and the new, grand one. And this needed to be pointed out, for Eileen continued to grow up.

Although Eileen was no longer a little girl, the old pursuits lost none of their excitement. She took to fishing by herself on the castle shores when Sandy was away at fairs or had taken a turn at road-making. Eileen could not tell whether she loved the setting of her lines the more, or the daydreaming while she waited for a bite. The castle had long seen the end of human habitation. The day when its last ceilings fell was remembered by none living. Even the fungi which crept along its rotten woodwork died because it had no more ancient oak to feast on. Spiders had no more dusty windowpanes to hang up their webs. Inlaid floors which some Georgian lord laid down for silk slippers to dance on had become open patches of earth where foxglove nodded with knapweed between the crumbling stone walls.

But Eileen hardly noticed the decay. As she wandered through the stone gateway, Eileen built the ruins and peopled the rooms. Where indignant rooks flew in the square open sky above a long-vanished gallery, Eileen saw paintings of ladies in fine clothes, like those in a book they once had at school. And though the rooks might caw around the groups of tall chimney pots, Eileen heard the voices of the builders who brought the stone from the quarry six miles away. Sandy said the castle was older than the railway, older than the Battle of Vinegar Hill. But for Eileen it was without age.

When the sun was low and glowed with false light through the gaping windows, Eileen was not afraid, not even when the tinker lads might be huddled in a corner cursing over the Devil's cards. The steps down to the cellars held no terrors and she loved their dank passages, lit here and there where the vaulting had collapsed and where the weeds were brightest and thickest. Thick too, were the walls down there. Eileen could imagine her father as one of the builders. She could picture him mixing the yellow beastings with the crimson, hot blood of bullocks to make the mortar of horsehair and lime. The immensity of the walls seemed even greater when she touched them or put her fingers into the cracks to pull out the embedded hairs.

Before wandering slowly back to her fishing by the shore where the round towers rose so strongly from the water, Eileen's castle was complete. Inside was the sound of rustling satins as a lady went gracefully among its rooms. And Eileen was the lady and her dress was of the finest, finer even than the shroud

which Uncle Reuben had bought himself on the church outing
to Bundoran.

When she and Big Sandy sat late by the fire he often asked
what thoughts made her eyes quiver, now with light, now with
the shade, like red-bellies in the river. But Eileen never told
him. She stirred the ashes and put in the pot-lid to heat, so that
she could wrap the bright red flannel round it, before taking it
up to warm her bed in the loft. Her father would not understand
about the castle. And for the same reason she did not tell him
about the mangel at Hallowe'en.

Eileen was ten, and at a Hallowe'en *ceili* the girls had been
blindfolded and sent into a neighbour's mangel field, for the
goats had made short work of their own turnips. The girls had to
pull up the first root they touched, for this mangel would show
what kind of husband they would have. And more than the
simple faith of her mother's God-house, or her father's belief in
the good luck spitting of fair days, or her own hope in the lumps
of coal she had thrown over her shoulder, Eileen trusted in what
the mangel foretold.

The size and soundness, the shape and good heart of the
mangel were all clear signs of their future husband's character
and fortune. Eileen was happy for there was not one at the *ceili*
who did not agree that hers was the bonniest root ever set in a
manger before the cloven beast.

Plainly, Eileen was destined for high places. No old, bald cattle
dealer for her, for the mangel had leaves galore. The root was
straight and almost without scar, except for a hoe-mark on one
side. Eileen cut it into tiny pieces and found no rot, and nothing
but goodness in every part. That her husband would be a good
man there was no doubt, neither that he would be rich. When
she pulled the mangel up, great lumps of earth still clung to it,
indicating riches that even she had not dared to dream about.

During the passing years Eileen was conscious of few changes
other than the slow progression of the seasons and the mangel's
prophecy. The sun's first touch would release the white nightcap
of old maid's strawberry and cause the crests and tippets of the

crane-duck to grow for his great courtship. And their cries of mating out on Hazzard's Lake would fill the gathering day with trumpet glory and moaning delight that had to be heard to be believed. But when spring had really settled and the redshanks flapped wings of love, and dry goats suddenly filled a score of porringers, then Eileen was happiest. Through the months ahead there would be no more dark nights to follow her dad through to his traps and snares. There would be no more falls of snow to blanket the woods when she went among the blackened trunks and branches to gather twigs, no more dazzling drifts along the verges where the gamekeeper could follow her spoor by the railway line.

This gamekeeper was a firm friend of Eileen's, for they often met when she was out with her father's terrier bitch, whom the gamekeeper held in admiration. In spite of having lost half a leg in a reaping machine, the terrier maintained her reputation as champion ratter at threshing time. Eileen always took the dog to the threshings herself, for she collected husks to soak for sowens. And for all the rats killed she was rewarded with a good stone of corn which came in handy for the bantam and her mother's leghorns. But though Sandy's dog was admired by the gamekeeper, Sandy himself was not. They were sworn enemies, for poachers were hated more than any travelling folk of the roadside. And Eileen was Big Sandy's guard, the shadow that fell into his footsteps through snow and hail.

But long before threshing was thought about, before she had made her dad a flax knot in his buttonhole for the harvest fair, there had been summer sun and such fish as only grasshoppers could lure out of the lake. Long days of dapping with no hindrances like school or the fetching of water followed each other, and long nights when the rudd of the far river never stopped biting. No long-eared owl took to the night hunt of bird or mammal as eagerly as Eileen and her dad climbed the heather hills in search of red grouse. And those were blessed wartime days when a man could go fowling seabirds for sale to the starving English. Eileen waded through the lakes' shady shallows, basket over her back, to collect gulls' eggs. The sharp-beaked birds swooped on her like dive-bombers, and round her brown legs the water lapped like velvet. Would she have to eat the fishy gulls' eggs like the English, when she was a lady, Eileen wondered, though she loved nothing better than a big green duck egg when she and her dad got home, thirsty for buttermilk, weary with pleasure.

None of this, it seemed, could ever change. Yet before Eileen was halfway through her last book at school, the great restlessness swamped her. It was inexplicable. She could locate the cause neither within nor outside herself. Nothing was satisfying any more. Things that had been beautiful before, became dull. With the single exception of her father, the family and her friends irritated her. The house seemed too small. The five trains a day which demanded the opening of the gates suddenly appeared to be unreasonable demands on her time and interest, although she could think of nothing she would rather do instead. Long after the others had settled to deep sleep, Eileen would lie in bed sighing like the weeping-ash beyond the shed where the railway oil was stored. And as the dawn winds gathered the young sallies together this way and that, Eileen tossed in the bed longing to be up and away.

If the family noticed the change in Eileen, they were good enough not to say so. And through it all Eileen's dream of the grand future remained constant. Fine silks to wear during a week consisting entirely of Sundays with herring teas and shop bread was still her idea of the perfect life. But meanwhile, the restlessness continued to canker her present life. Taking the goats along the verges, once her favourite pastime, now became a burden hardly to be borne. Eileen shouted at the innocent goats and forbade them to climb the foxglove cuttings on the way. For the first time in her life, one afternoon, she even used her dad's blackthorn on them when they pulled her up the steepest bank for the windfalls of an orphan summerjohn.

This tree stood along the railway line like some lonely-bush. And to call it so was no exaggeration, for under its knotted limbs the ghost of Mary Price had appeared to many a lad as he went a-snaring. Eileen, however, had no more patience with spectres than she had for flesh and blood just at that particular time. Only herself interested her. There was no pride in seeing the meadows cut clean to the living earth, no joy in weaving split sally rods into creels for her dad's secret use. And how she hated having to go up to the crossroads for linseed oil cake to put the calves in fine fettle for the fair.

So deep did the disturbance go that Eileen began to regard it as normal and permanent. As often as possible she fled the house for the dark pine plantations. Thoughts about destiny pursued her, driving her frantic as though, like the summer cattle, she was possessed of the cleg madness. One idea seemed to emerge clearly from all the confusion. She must get away from the railway dwelling and the level-crossing folk who surrounded her, crushing her freedom, cramping her style. But where should she go? It was not impossible to run away to Belfast and go into service. Or perhaps she could go to Enniskillen and work in a shop.

It was out of the question that she should go down the railway line to bake and sew for Uncle Reuben now that he had taken to his bed. It was all very well for him to cling on to life so that he could boast about being a hundred years old. But when Eileen had carried him down a sight of scones he had thrown them at her because there was no snuff with them. And Eileen could not bear to hear all over again his stories about the cow-heads they used to have in his boyhood, and the fiddle dances that were held in the forge before even her father was born. She wanted to set her own feet tapping, rather than see the dust kicked up by ghosts. She wanted to be carried off somewhere, and to be anywhere but at the level-crossing or the decaying forge.

A relief came when she gave a tinker woman a setting of bantam eggs so that she would read her hand. The woman foretold such marvellous things that for months afterwards a glow of happiness returned, as though her earth-heavy mangel had been found all over again. Eileen left school at this time. The four eldest of the family were all out working and bringing in a bit for the housekeeping, so Eileen saw that she must stay at home and keep the level-crossing gates. As suddenly as it had come, the restlessness left her. Everyone remarked how quickly Eileen seemed to have grown into a young woman, although she was gone eighteen before a man asked if he might walk her home from the harvest thanksgiving.

Eileen discovered she liked his attentions very much but the man himself very little. So shortly afterwards she allowed herself to be walked home by another. But Eileen was still her dad's darling and he had no intentions of letting her go to any weaving lad or lonely byreman. Under these conditions it looked as if his daughter would be well into her twenties still without a decision being made in favour of this or that man. However, the tinker woman's reading had to be fulfilled—'when death crosses your path,' she had prophesied, 'then the glory will follow'.

Not wishing to risk her reputation as a seer, the tinker had refused to say whose death or exactly what the glory would be. So when the old master died up at the mansion house neither Eileen nor her mother could tell for certain whether this could be the death referred to. On hearing about the funeral arrangements they both came to the conclusion that this *must* be the death, for the procession was certain to cross their path, literally, by coming over the level-crossing. It was to do so long before the last cattle train was due in the afternoon, the slackest period of a slack day. And when she heard about the grand arrangements Eileen was thankful that long ago she had insisted on changing out of her old pinny when she went out to the crossing.

After opening and closing the gates she liked to linger a while gossiping with the farmers going to and fro to the fair and town. And she could never tell whether the country horticulturist or the young curate would pass by and lift their hats. It would mortify her to be seen in her milking pinny. The master's funeral, Eileen decided, demanded even more than a change of pinny. So she put on her Sunday dress. Her presence was necessary at the gate, not only out of respect but in order to count the wreaths, because the master had been a great Orangeman.

Around the appointed time Eileen and her mother were
standing by the crossing. They looked anxiously up the road
along which the cortège should come. Mother and daughter
relieved each other periodically and went indoors to have a cup
of tea, but there was no sign of the funeral. Darkness threatened
before long. Eileen's mother grew edgy. In addition to the
funeral there had been a small back-end fair that day with much
cattle on the roads. At last someone came down from the
mansion house bearing the news that the old master had given a
last message to the gathered mourners by inconsiderately
exploding in his coffin, whereupon he had had to be specially
sealed in with lead.

Eileen was in the garden getting a few shallots in for the
dinner her dad would have after the fair, when she saw the
funeral coming round the corner. It was a very stylish affair
indeed, with motorcars from Belfast and quality from as far as the
south lands of Cavan. And in spite of all the timing and waiting,
was not the gate against them and a sight of bullocks and ass-
carts from the tail-end of the fair halted on the farther side.
Eileen recalled how the old master flew into tempers when he
was on a pleasure outing and found the level-crossing against
him. She hoped that he would not burst his lead coffin with
annoyance now, right on their doorstep.

At last the ground trembled, and the rails sang and the wires
jangled and the cattle train puffed laboriously into sight. Plainly
it had no intention of hurrying, old master or no old master.
And just for sheer cussedness it had more wagons than was
usual, more it seemed, than even there were wreaths on the
hearse. While she followed each rumbling wagon and its
moaning, roan load, Eileen's eye alighted on a young man. He
stood close to the gate, looking quite unsuitably cheerful for a
funeral; in fact, Eileen decided, he was distinctly amused. He
was about twenty, exquisitely dressed and clearly belonged to
the mansion house family. But Eileen was fairly certain that he
was not the new young master who had once come to the red
velvet box-pew in the church.

Behind the young man's amused glance, which flitted lightly from the train to the hearse, from family to the mourners and then back again, there was something else. The pale face and full, blood-red lips held an expression quite different from the hale and ruddy cheeks of the other young men in bowler hats. His skin, like fresh creamery butter, suggested that he never indulged in rough games or hunting, which she knew the others did. Fully occupied with these thoughts, the passing train and funeral alike forgotten, Eileen stood staring at the young man. Then he turned suddenly, as though she had called to him, and looked into her eyes. For a moment, neither of them moved. Then, quite deliberately, he gave her a slow, solemn but wicked wink.

Confused and blushing, Eileen opened the level-crossing gates, leaving the funeral to sort itself out with the bullocks and ass-carts. When she recovered her composure, and embarrassment stole away with guilt, the young man's face did not fade from her mind as she had expected. Instead, its handsome lines and strange expression came before her like a phantom.

During the rest of the day her mother enquired what possessed Eileen, for she did not hear when anyone spoke to her, broke two plates, and, for the first time in her life, forgot to light the gate lamp. After the evening milking when her mother insisted on going up to the graveyard to read the wreath cards, Eileen complied, for nothing, just then, could take the image away.

During the weeks afterwards, people's gossip concerned itself with little else than the fortune of money which the old master left besides his domain and herds. But Eileen spoke to no one of what the funeral had meant to her.

A hard winter set in. The goats ran dry earlier than usual, and twites searched the barren fields that were fastnesses of ice for weeks on end. It was Boxing Day that Eileen got up from the fire, and wrapped herself warmly and took the goats out, because now that the quality were abroad celebrating Christmas with guns, not a stake in the county could keep the goats from bolting. To save going out for fuel again that day, into the raw cold, Eileen began to collect wood for the fire and to tie the sticks together with the belt from her rainproof. As she unbent from her task she found Mr. Guy, for that was the name of the young man in the funeral procession who had winked at her. He had suddenly appeared from somewhere and was standing right beside her. He was so close that she could almost feel his breath on her cheek.

Sensations seized her that she had never known existed. The face that she had longed so often to see again, moved her even more than before, now that it was so near. In the eyes she read joy, a triumph in seeing her again, that perfectly matched her own feelings. For the briefest of moments she thought he was going to chide her for taking wood from his cousin's plantation. By dint of discreet enquiries Eileen had found out his name and the fact that he was the new master's cousin. He must be over to spend Christmas at the mansion house.

But Guy said not a word about the bundle of wood, and in fact took it from her, and insisted on carrying it all the way back to the railway dwelling with her.

'After all,' he said at once grandly and kindly, 'walking with you is better than rushing with a blasted gun.'

Eileen was too shy to attempt much of an answer, and besides, she was worried lest they run into the gamekeeper and he should make some untoward comments about the wood. Half afraid that Guy was able to read her thoughts she glanced up at him as he chatted merrily away with no purpose in mind but to make himself mightily agreeable to her. For there had not been a day since the funeral when he had not in some way or other thought of the young girl at the level-crossing. And what he had not been able to explain for the life of him was that this time he had mentioned her to nobody. Usually, he boasted and exaggerated about his amorous activities. Had this railway girl been any one of the other hundreds he had done no more than wink at, he would have retailed a fantastically elaborated version, hinting at all sorts of ungallant but very gentlemanly deeds.

When he saw the look on Eileen's face he changed the bundle of wood to the other hand and caught her fingers in his. It seemed so natural, so right that Eileen felt as if they had always done this together, all their lives.

'You know, I have thought of nobody but you since that day,' Guy said. This was not strictly true, but at that moment he ardently believed it was. With unconditional surrender, Eileen said that her mind too had been consumed by thoughts of him. They parted at the railway dwelling's gate, he leaning on it chin in hand, boring into her like a gimlet with his eyes, she awkwardly clutching the bundle which he had carried for a while, as though it were a golden fleece her Jason had brought.

'First rate!' he exclaimed, thumping the top bar of the gate when Eileen agreed for him to come with his sports car and take her up to St. Lasser's Cell by Claddagh Bridge for a spin.

It is not true marriage but true love which is made in heaven. That is why the former can be, and frequently is, broken (in deed, if not in name), but the latter never. Eileen at least was in no doubt that she had found her life's secret. Suddenly, the whole of her days assumed the simplest and most beautiful of meanings. She saw that, quite plainly, all the delicacy of feeling which distinguished her from other members of her faily, all the daydreaming she had indulged in about silks to wear and grand houses to live in were solely directed towards fitting her as a companion for Guy. For Eileen had not the slightest doubt but that he would ask for her hand.

And within the week, of course, the news of such goings-on was had by every crossroads in the barony. The old master's funeral dropped immediately to a place as a reserve topic for talk. Big Sandy's girl and the new young master's cousin from over the water! Eileen McFinn and Mr. Guy.

Meanwhile the bare-twigged lanes echoed to the roar of the sports car, the naked woods crackled underfoot to the tramp of lovers' feet, the curtains at many a mansion house window moved surreptitiously as a maid followed the silhouette of two figures walking arm-in-arm down the long drive.

Big Sandy was bowled over. He loved Eileen. To have her snatched away from him so suddenly and completely, bewildered him. And in addition there was the astounding fact that a McFinn was about to become one of the quality. Had she been taken up to heaven like Elijah in his chariot, Big Sandy would not have been so amazed. Certainly Eileen would not have been so remote as she soon would be. Within a very short time no question remained as to whether Guy would marry Eileen or not. He stood his ground bravely. His own father raved and threatened to cut him off but Guy remained adamant. And Big Sandy bowed to fate's blow.

Eileen's dad had always planned big things for her. No common serving boy or roadmender was going to carry off *his* favourite girl. Sandy's intentions for her levelled themselves at somebody like a seed-merchant or a farmer with enough outwintering stock to keep a herdman of his own. But Eileen's marriage into the quality was almost beyond his comprehension. How could she ever begin to understand a young man like Mr. Guy who belonged to that strange world where people could neither count their bullocks nor had ever known the power of their milk cheque. Although he could point to no particular objection, he considered that the marriage was not right, neither now nor in the future. His contemplations were too deep and tender to be trusted with words, so he remained silent in his corner by the fire. When Eileen spared an hour or so to be away from Guy and was about the house again, Sandy sat looking at her like a sad spaniel. But Eileen's joy blinded her. She did not notice the mute appeal in her father's face.

Dumbly, Big Sandy allowed himself to be measured and fitted out with a new suit to see Eileen off for her grand wedding in England. For a week before her departure the railway dwelling had been in an uproar. Guy called constantly and Sandy had to admit he was a decent young fellow who would never see a man stuck for the price of a lump of tobacco. Eileen's mother quite lost her head over her son-in-law to-be. On several occasions Sandy was obliged to speak sharply to her, telling her not to be a silly woman.

Right up to the day when she went away, Big Sandy could

find no fault with Guy. Eileen had obtained in every way what she had wanted from life. And Sandy and his wife would also benefit from the match. No sooner would Eileen be married than they would have every travelling grocer at their door and every windfall tree without the asking. Within the twelvemonth her sister would be courting a two-byre farmer and Jimmy the nestlecock doing the books at the creamery. Nothing but good could come of it all.

Yet Sandy was still not happy about the marriage. Guy might have the looks and manners and clothes of a gentleman, he might speak with a voice of honey, and be a good crack with a gun, but, and this was the question he could not answer, would he make his Eileen a good mate?

Eileen took quickly to her new life. Even before they took up residence in England after their honeymoon, she was quite transformed. It pleased her to wield the power of wealth, and as though born to such things, gracious living came easily. Now that they were over, Guy's bride felt no regrets for the days when there had been more dinner-times than dinners. She felt no homesickness for the wells which ran dry, or for the pet pigs which needed suckling in the night.

Her behaviour was by nature that of a lady, and although she pretended to no great claims whenever the subject of her family was raised, she did resort to some exaggeration, in order to avoid persistent questioners. Her father, she explained, had been stationmaster. Though some of the people to whom she said this tittered with embarrassment, to Eileen the rank of stationmaster had always been an exalted one. He had not only worn a billycock and dickie every day of the week, but had each year been the judge of the best level-crossing garden, and in her old life these were high honours.

Guy gallantly shielded his wife from the more cruel of his friends. He cut his own social life to the bone and dropped anyone whom he thought would bait Eileen with her background and upbringing. And being by nature gentle and graceful, she did not take long to learn the essential mannerisms required of her new position. Snobbery and the more refined forms of social behaviour never concerned her.

Nothing clouded their bright days. Not even the most besotted of Guy's circle could refuse to acknowledge that Eileen was a beauty. When the first child was born, son and heir, Guy's parents capitulated. Prejudice against the mother of such a grandson could at least be modified. Eileen's sister crossed from Ireland to be with her at the birth. Eileen was surprised to find she was not as comforted by this as she thought she would be. And when the sister went back again loaded with presents for the railway family, Eileen felt no pangs. She realised then that the old life could never be reconciled with the new.

Eileen had no regrets, except those which arose when she faced the fact that her youth was over. Guy made her happy and four more children were born. Guy's father came round to speak of her as 'a damn good girl'. Her sons worshipped their mother, for Eileen taught them how to fish and how to spit in the first trout's mouth. And she surrounded those hours by the river with an exciting sense of mystery, for they were never to say unlucky words, such as 'sow' or 'priest' or 'pin' while they were setting their lines.

Eileen grew to a new loveliness. Occasionally, on a lonely afternoon walk through the woods, she would slip off her shoes and stockings just to feel the earth's freshness against her bare feet, as she had done in the old days. Pining could never resurrect the past. Had she denied Guy and remained in Ireland for the rest of her life, she would have mourned him in her heart. Bowing to the finality of events, Eileen did not return to her old home for many years.

Her sister's was the only visit from the family, and at first Eileen sent and received more letters than ever Guy knew. But with five children of her own, she had enough worries. Each Christmas found a growing list of Irish nephews and nieces who must have presents. Apart from this there was little news exchanged. Times were bad in West Ulster. Then she heard that the railway had already been closed for a number of years, and soon afterwards news came of her mother's death.

Eileen felt a bleak wind blow across the landscape of her life. The railway had been the heart of her existence up to the meeting with Guy. She had never imagined that it too could die as her mother had done. Her parents had long ago given up the dwelling at the level-crossing and had moved into another cottage with a decent garden. With a shock, Eileen counted up and found that twenty years had slipped by. And this thought filled her on the journey home for the funeral.

She came to her father's house and the place was full of people whom she did not know. But there was a wake. Not a crumb of cheese could be seen nor a slice of ham. No fiddler played in the corner, there were no hammer games or riddles, no dancing nor a single prank of the old wake gatherings. Eileen saw at once that the Pilgrims were in charge with lots of hymns and testimonies. Her sister Molly was giving out Gospel tracts to unbelievers and had her own hair done up in a Christian bun. And when Eileen peered into the open coffin, she saw that her mother's face was serene and that one hand clasped a fat Bible. Nobody would dare put salt into that coffin, just as no one dared ask for the bunion charm secret on her deathbed.

Eileen looked round at the crowd of odd scrubbed, Christian faces, and was happy that her father was not among them. He at least, she felt sure, had not changed. Eileen could hardly believe that this was her family's home, and she went outside.

From the August meadows, she could hear the reapers working on into the night. She remembered that this was the daddy-long-legs season. Her father would probably be away over at the lake after trout, or perhaps he had gone, as the old custom was, to tell the bees about his wife's homing spirit. Picking her way carefully, wonder filling her at the beauty of the countryside, Eileen came to the deserted level-crossing. The first thing she noticed was the big wooden post. The nearer gate used to swing on it. As a child she thought no bigger or stronger post could ever be found, and that a team of horses could be tethered there and not move it. To this post she herself had tethered innumerable broody hens so that the crows should not steal the chicks. Now the post was rotten, and its pulpy heart sported the fleshy flanges of dryad's saddle.

Eileen looked at the railway lines. The steely-bright, shining rails that had run the breadth of two counties were barely discernible. A few rusty lengths appeared here and there where the usurping mares-tails had not completely overrun the track. Eileen pushed open the railway dwelling's door. It was not locked, nor ever had been during the whole of her childhood. But she could feel nothing for this dank, forlorn stone box. Weeds grew through its floor, though it sounded hollow enough, as though the skulls of the four horses, planted for foundations under each corner, were still watchful of the family's luck. And surely the warm kitchen that she remembered had not been this airless, tiny room. Had they all really slept in the loft, at the head of that mouldering ladder, fighting to lie nearest the warm chimney-stack? But the derelict house conveyed nothing. No tentacles reached out to suck her into the past.

With amusement Eileen saw that, after all, the place had not been completely abandoned. The big hole in the wall by the fire had once been used for keeping the salt. Now a row of tins stood there with oddments whose purpose was known only to the poacher. But Eileen identified the rush band at once, crumbling and broken though it was. She had made it for her dad when he sprained his wrist. That had been the autumn when the boundary oak was blown across the railway line. To help her dad clear it, she was given two whole days from school. And there had been a third holiday when they borrowed O'Brien's harlequin mare and took the trunk to the mill. And then, when her dad sprained his wrist, she sat tending the goats, weaving the green rushes into the band that was now brown and lifeless in the salt-hole.

Eileen recognised the other things as odd bits of her dad's fishing tackle—the top of a mud-spear, the old cocoa-tin for the grasshoppers, the horsehair that might yet be threaded through the dusty bundle of swan quills. Unexpectedly then, on seeing these oddments, emotions seized her. Memories crowded in.

There had been the yellow eel nights taken on long lines, the setting of coghill nets, the song of the weirs, the glinting of trout, and brutes of pike in the far river. Eileen understood why her dad came back to the railway dwelling, and why the salt-hole had at last been claimed as his secret hiding place.

But the chain of lakes would be unaltered by twenty years. The grand rivers would flow on for ever. Woods still rang with crowing pheasants, and the water-meadows still echoed to the hoarse rasp of the snipe. At her own home in England there was a lake, with enough waterfowl for the taking, and there were trout to which Big Sandy was more than welcome. But Eileen saw now why her father would not accept her invitations. His sport was not so much the fishing and snaring as it was the defying of peelers and the outraged quality. His pleasure was the skilful avoiding and deceiving of water-bailiffs, stewards and gamekeepers. Gaffing the salmon or loopnetting the trout was nothing at all if the law was on his side.

Eileen fingered the swan quills and held them to her nose for the old familiar, fishy-musty smell. What feather fishing they had enjoyed in the last of many a sunset amongst the whirlpools of the river bends or the feeding grounds of the horse-fords. Then she put the quills back in the salt-hole and went out, pulling the door behind her. Great stillness brooded over the countryside. It was indeed the best of evenings for the trout beyond Reuben's old forge. She began to walk along the disused track, where the goats had once tugged her. But near the plantation she halted. At the top of the bank she saw a man clambering through the fence. The trees' shadow was dense, now that the young firs she had known were grown nobly and were ready for cutting. What sport the local girls will have, she thought, when the woodsmen come and set up their little huts.

Moving with the stealth of a wild animal, the man scrambled down the bank, then stood by the railway line, dusting the seat of his trousers. Then, like some badger just out of his sett, he ambled off along the track. In his hands was a large fish. As he went by, Eileen, standing in the gloom of a bush, saw that every hair of her father's head was white. He passed near enough for her to see his eyes, twinkling with excitement at this latest bit of poaching.

She waited for Big Sandy to get twenty yards away. Then she laughed and ran after him. There was no fuss or strain.

'You rascal,' were his first words, 'you fair scared the daylights out of me.' Then, 'What d'ye think of this?' Held up the trout. It was every ounce of ten pounds.

The twenty vanished years seemed like no time at all. It might have been only yesterday that they last walked side by side along the track. Neither of them felt any need to talk, not even about the dead woman. Sandy began to sing softly:

With a hunting bitch that will not whine,
A heifer's milk within me,
Seven landlords' water will be mine,
And a hare on every lea.

Tattoo Lily

THEY WERE NO MERE ACCIDENTS THAT caused God to give Mrs. Delham a fine head of orange-red hair, and Lily for a Christian name. From the beginning the Almighty must have had the plan in His head for making her a leader of His Protestant sheep and a holy terror to the Catholic goats. Papishes were coming over the border to buy up good Protestant land for miles around the countryside. Lily herself could name the two best wells in the neighbourhood which were now polluted by falling into Catholic hands. But in spite of such losses on the flanks, the main spearhead of Lily's attack went forward undaunted. She ruled supreme and there wasn't a Prod to be met with anywhere who could match the ardour of her great Orange soul.

Lily was known in both camps as Tattoo Lily. Her body was supposed to be completely covered with tattooed devices explaining in detail the secrets of the Orange ABC. The truth of this widely held belief had never been verified, not even by Tattoo Lily's own Lodge brethren. Almost the only evidence which could lend weight was an extant photograph owned by a tattoo artist off Sandy Row. Though now faded it showed Lily

receiving the needle and a half-formed Union Jack appearing on
her exposed forearm. This flag was reputed to be the first tattoo
of the famous series which came afterwards. Once begun, of
course, such a tradition could not be suppressed. It was not
uncommon to hear Ribbonmen and Orange blades alike joking
about the mystical 'I' that stood for the Israelites who 'crossed
sweet Jordan's streams'. There were said to be so many of these
escaping figures tattooed on Lily's stomach that 'Hard K for
Knox' could hardly find standing room for his truth. Moreover,
Tattoo Lily wore thick woollen stockings even when marching
to the Field on the Twelfth and these were thought to be a
cover-up for the remaining Orange symbols which descended to
her very feet. Lily's tattoos and her manner of concealing them
gave rise to as many theories as there were about Queen
Alexandra (of glorious and pious memory) and the great pearl
choker which hid her neck from the public gaze.

No traveller could go to that part of Ulster without coming
across Tattoo Lily in some way or another. Many people indeed
made a special journey just to see her, a kind of pilgrimage. The
garden of her cottage was itself a sight worth seeing. This was
particularly so in summer when Tattoo Lily sat in it surrounded
by a fine array of Protestant flowers. She always sat in the same
place in the same chair and received men and women from all
walks of life who represented Orange or Purple or Black Lodges
of the secret society. It was common knowledge, and probably
true too, that Sir Edward Carson had given her his photograph
and had walked to the Field on the Twelfth of July wearing in
his buttonhole an orange lily that had come from her garden.

But the flowers were nothing when compared with the
topiary, which fenced her bright garden about. Not even the
sweet williams of every possible colour and combination of
colour could vie with the green, sculptured shapes of Tattoo
Lily's hedges and shrubs. Long years of clipping and training had
produced a noble sight indeed, another panoply of symbols
representing the Protestant faith. There were stars of David,
lions of Judah, Arks of the Covenant, British Crowns Imperial,

coffins, ladders, tools and arches and a score of miscellaneous items depicting esoteric lore known only to the Orange Institution. Such an extravagance of the topiarist's art might seem to have been born to waste its sweetness. But nothing of the sort was the case. Tattoo Lily's cottage, far from being isolated, was served by a second-class country road. On fair days a constant stream of traffic went by, on foot, on horseback, and in an astonishing variety of wheeled conveyances. There were men and women and children and animals in such a richness of life and movement that would render the Parthenon's frieze a bauble by comparison. Long before dawn, droves of donkeys came down from the mountains, bullocks and springing cows, bold Billy Boys and gumptionless Free Staters, tinkers and half-gentry all on their way to sell or be sold. And they all, every single man-jack of them, had to pass the sermon-cum-speech in Tattoo Lily's topiary.

By her seventh sense, her Orange one, Tattoo Lily would know if one of the other side was passing. Her own people always showed the greatest respect for the hedge, some of the more regular passers-by even touched their caps on reaching the yew carved as an enormous British Crown. But there could be no telling what outrage the Fenians would commit if Wycliffe, her little son, was not out in the front banging his Orange drum and holding the fort. Tattoo Lily knew too well what she might find on fair days if the garden was left unprotected. There had been the Catholic drover from the Border whom she had spotted crouching under the box hedge about to perform his natural functions. To the innocent this may sound a perfectly reasonable thing for a drover to do, quietly and discreetly in the shadow of a hedge that would certainly come to no harm at all. But that particular box was Lily's *pièce de résistance*, being a fine clump of trees, high and close cut at the top with a stonemason's precision into battlements. It represented the Walls of Jericho. Without taking thought but only action, Lily managed to fire her shotgun over the man's head in time to save the holy bush from desecration. The drover toppled over backwards in his confusion and was observed to be fleeing at a speed only slightly less than that of light, a difference of velocity brought about mainly by his trousers which he did not stop to hitch up. This was a test case, and in the event proved highly successful. Tattoo Lily could only presume that word must have circulated quickly amongst potential Fenian invaders that she was a determined and dangerous woman. This was a correct conclusion for the Catholics to come to, for indeed she was. Appeasement was a political method unknown to her—at any rate she was never obliged again to have recourse to the shotgun.

It was not to be expected, of course, that minor incidents and annoyances would cease altogether. Tattoo Lily would have felt at a loss if they had. On another fair day after the drover's visit the boys from the chapel crossroad got up to their Papish schemes. They tried to stick the tricolour of the South into the large clipped Crown that represented such freedom to the North. But on this occasion also Tattoo Lily was able to confound their knavish tricks. Because the Crown grew at the gable end of the house and the bantam cock roosted in the lower branches with his harem, she had ample warning of the assault. The boys had thought to steal the march on Tattoo Lily by coming at first light on their way to the fair, before Lily was awake. But they had reckoned without that Protestant bantam. Quick as lightning Lily's hand reached under the bed and she was at the window. For weeks afterwards people round about discussed the great aim Lily had, whether it be with chamberpot or gun.

Lily was not so foolish as to imagine that her garden contained the whole world. Her loyalty carried her far beyond the topiary hedges, the sweet williams and orange lilies. An excess of missionary spirit sent her travelling all over the country to Lodge meetings and socials. Besides her exemplary loyalty and zeal, a fine, strong, though to be truthful not always tuneful, voice made her acceptable at any of these functions. After a few experiments in her early years when Tattoo Lily tried to sing in choirs it was tactfully suggested that her voice was too powerful and that she could best serve the cause as a soloist. On a number of occasions when Lily had sung in choirs and noted people or the local gentry were in attendance, the conductors or church organists had afterwards been put to considerable embarrassment. They were complimented on the performance and told what a fine soloist they had, when, in fact, the choral works contained no passages for solo voice at all. In general, however, Lily remained oblivious of any musical *faux pas* she might make and after branching out on her own no ambiguous interpretation could be put on an evening's entertainment.

Lily might be bad at singing but she was never boring. Her repertoire was inexhaustible, and though strictly limited to songs with a strong, not to say biased, Protestant flavour, it contained every Orange song ever written. Some people, who did not approve of Tattoo Lily as much as they ought to have done, even maintained that the repertoire included songs that had never been written. Comments such as these were apt to be forthcoming from the more strait-laced in the community who found fault with Lily's habit of consuming a full bottle of Bushmills whiskey during the course of one evening. Her critics were inflamed even more by the fact that they could not level against her their usual teetotallers' charge concerning loss of finer judgement, loss of exact speech, loss of limb control and loss of propriety. Tattoo Lily just simply never got drunk. The fiery liquor went down merely to inspire her singing with a new verve.

By and large, Tattoo Lily was above criticism. After such a gathering she was always in a fit state to light the carbon lamp on her bicycle and cycle home. Nobody ever found her under a hedge, having fallen off her bicycle. Perhaps the only symptom of the Bushmills was that Lily would not stop singing. Once the concert or dance was done and the last applause had died in the rafters (a structural feature which local newspapers claimed rang with applause), she would still go on singing. Along the country lanes feebly lit by the bicycle lamp she would sing, past haunted houses and babbling brooks she would sing and so to the second-class country road and the familiar, soul-stirring silhouette of her own topiary. Lily would still be humming to herself as sleep

overcame her. There was never any difficulty in getting her to
start, but only in stopping her.

There was then, no reason in the world why anyone should
have advised Lily to be careful on the roads. And neither was
there any reason why, on that particular morning, she should
have had any premonition as she climbed on to her bicycle. A
small fair was going on in the neighbouring town that day and
Tattoo Lily wanted to get there early, not because of the things
being sold but because of the people. Lily had a mission to fulfil
and its success depended on large numbers of people because
she was collecting signatures for a petition. She bowled along
the country road, bosom swelling with Protestant pride and the
rightness and righteousness of what she had undertaken. The
petition, when completed, would go to the King himself. Its
strong wording attested by hundreds of Orange signatures,
would voice a protest against the visit to the Pope by a member
of the Royal Family. Although Tattoo Lily had not yet actually
penned the petition, its form was already present in her mind.
Grand sonorous phrases would pile up one on another like a
fugue. Words like 'humble and most obedient servants', 'loyal
subjects', and 'slavery to Rome' would appear in Lily's petition.
At this point it must be made plain that Lily never once
consciously sought self-glory or aggrandisement. Her efforts for
King and country were always ingenuous, and the petition
touched on matters very near to her heart. So once arrived at
the fair she flung herself body and soul into the matter and
before the first heifers had been sold, dozens of signatures were
down, and long before the first luck-penny was spent, Lily had
collected over a hundred.

Not all the petitioners were sure what, in fact, Lily was
blathering about. By mid-morning many of them were so drunk
that they would not have cared anyway even if they had known.
But as Tattoo Lily was reckoned to be a great sport of a woman
and champion of any good cause, they obligingly signed their
names on the line where her finger pointed. A great number of
others thought that Lily had something to do with the buying

and selling and so, of course, she got involved with the drinking of whiskies over the luck-pennies. As she passed from group to group with her bits of paper, more and more farmers invited her to take a wee drop, which in a lot of cases was not so wee either. After what seemed only an hour or so Lily was a little surprised to find that evening had come on and that the fair was rapidly breaking up. However, a satisfactory wadge of paper now crinkled with hundreds of signatures was compensation enough.

The first sign Lily had that anything was amiss was when she could not remember where she had left her bicycle. A short search revealed it leaning outside the public bar of Dan O'Connell's, but by then she realised that a drop too much had passed her lips. How Lily wished that she had gone petitioning by pony and trap, for now she could simply have climbed aboard and let the beast lead her home. In a decidedly uncertain fashion, Lily pedalled out of the town watched with professional interest by the policeman whose signature she had twice collected at different times earlier in the day. It was only on account of Lily letting him put his name down in two places, which he regarded as a special privilege, that he refrained from cautioning her about dangerous driving. Tattoo Lily was obviously going home and would soon be beyond the reach of his beat so should she come a cropper it would be somebody else's responsibility.

Lily managed very well, although she thought the young moon rolled about like a slice of scooped melon on a plate. So it did, for clusters of woolly clouds crept across its pale face, giving the moon a gliding motion it did not possess. But the rolling was all Lily's. The swimming sensation in her orange head did not altogether displease her, now that she had got used to it. And so she knew that light shining from the old mill was not an hallucination, but the glow of oil lamps. Lily knew that a new family had moved in during the week. Feeling so satisfied with her day's achievement, Lily thought it a fine opportunity to call and collect a few last names, before making the final lap home. Some years had passed since Tattoo Lily's previous visit to the mill, but she remembered the way round to the mill lodge and the precariously narrow bridge over the water that led to its door.

As she crossed this bridge, a curious presentiment of danger ahead pierced the screen of alcohol which closely guarded her senses. From an upstairs window she caught a series of intoned mumblings, first a solo mumble, followed by a chorus of mumbles. The pattern of antiphony repeated endlessly like a swarm of bees. Lily realised at once that the people of the house were at the Devil's beads. Hearing a recitation of the rosary in that house shocked Tattoo Lily, for many was the tuneful hour she had spent there in years gone by. The miller of her childhood had been a big Orangeman and a relative of the Grand Master himself. Unable to contain herself any longer, Lily let out her own voice at full blast. None was a stronger believer than herself in the power of song as a weapon against the papists. Was it not the Lillibullero that had sung James the Fleeing out of three kingdoms? So Tattoo Lily took a deep breath and as loud as she could gave them a good bleat of *The Sprigs of Kilrea:*

> *Then hurray and hurray for the sons of King William,*
> *And down with offenders where ever youse be,*
> *You may stop counting beads and quit midnight parades*
> *And put on Orange shoes when you come to Kilrea.*

Feeling that short of throwing a bomb through the window she had done her duty, Tattoo Lily fled down the hill on her bicycle, shouting Protestant battle songs and feeling elated with Boyne and Aughrim pride. And apart from this episode Tattoo Lily could remember not another thing of that evening. At the bottom of the hill the cycle threw her with a frightful crash. A passer-by found her an hour later still unconscious, head hanging backwards in the ditch, the petition papers lying strewn on the road. When hospitals, doctors, and the like had done with her Lily was trussed up in a wheelchair like a chicken ready for the oven. Neither she nor anybody else could make head nor tail out of the long names they gave her injuries, though she expressed great indignation when she heard *hysterical paraplegia* mentioned, for Lily was no eejit. Sufficient was it that she could not move without her wheels. Yet true to character Tattoo Lily emerged from her accident more of a hero than ever.

In connection with the accident it was soon discovered that a dog frightened by Lily's approach had dashed across the road, and that it was no dog at all, but a Papish red setter bitch obviously trained by the Jesuits.

This in itself was almost sufficient to earn Lily a martyrdom, but when the efforts of her day's petitioning resulted in the British princess postponing her visit to the Vatican, many people proclaimed that she was a martyr indeed. And like the saints exalted in heaven freed from the trammels of the body, Tattoo Lily found herself more in demand than ever before, and she covered more miles, visited more farms and parish halls than ever she had done on her own two legs. To crown her glory she was carried away down to Belfast to ride in an open landau to Finaghy Field. And at that great Twelfth of July meeting four of the finest members of parliament personally lifted Lily on to the platform for all the mighty throng to see and hear. The only regrets which Lily suffered because of her injury resulted from her inability to stand to attention every night when the BBC closed down with the national anthem. In time, however, this was put right when gracious permission was given for Lily simply to raise her right hand, an idea said to have originated with old Lord Craigavon.

Like life itself, these happenings vanished into a perspective of years becoming news no longer but only an accepted part of Ulster existence. Nobody ever thought of Tattoo Lily afterwards as anything other than an extremely lively woman in a wheelchair. The popping of the chair's motor was heard now along country lanes where before only the silent swish of bicycle tyres had disturbed the song thrushes and linnets. Far from fading out of the Orange scene, Lily continued to militate against Fenian intrigues and generally to tilt at Catholic windmills. From time to time fresh stories about her were circulated, each of which added to her fame. For a time the whole country talked about her orange lilies again. They were supposed to be flourishing in the window-boxes of Buckingham Palace, having been specially ordered from Tattoo Lily's garden so that the House of Windsor could show to the world how Protestant it was.

During these following years not the least significant event was that Wycliffe was growing up. Lustier than the lustiest plants in his mother's garden as he passed from boyhood to adolescence and touched the borders of manhood. Many considered him to be full of book-learning for in spite of his fresh, country robustness Wycliffe did read a great deal and was inclined to keep himself to himself. Much of his time passed in lonely wanderings over the hills and through the woods or simply sitting on the banks of streams gazing into the water. Wycliffe was a dreamer but he confided his dreams to nobody. Like the branches of trees that stooped low over brooks and caught at floating leaves and petals, Wycliffe collected a number of girlfriends. But like the floating leaves, they soon got free, and then he waited for the next.

Although not given to energetic pursuits and though he was never heard to express violent opinions about the Orange cause as his mother did, Wycliffe was well liked. He had no enemies and many friends, so one and all were proud but truly sorry when they heard he had taken the King's shilling. The war had only just got into its stride and Hitler was still plucking the countries of Europe as though they were mere ripe fruits on a tree. On the day that Wycliffe went away half the town turned out to see him on the train for Omagh where he would do his training. And this auspicious occasion was marked afterwards by observant people as the moment when it all began. From then on, they said, the rebels in Dublin began to scheme in collaboration with Rome itself for Lily's destruction. The rebels were credited with enough diabolical intelligence to know that Ireland would never be united and the Orange sash banished for ever, while Lily lived. And those people who remembered Wycliffe's going away recalled in later years that no Christian soul who had ever drunk a toast to the sacred memory of King Billy had ever dreamt or suspected the Fenian intrigue to undo Tattoo Lily. The Devil had more than a hand in it, they said, and Maynooth might well have been the brain behind the outrage which befell her.

Training complete, Wycliffe crossed the water and was soon in London. The famous streets rang to the pounding of his boots, and not a sight did he see but that a copious account of it was not sent home to Lily. Such grandeur there was in London, she told her friends, and proceeded to read them aloud every single word of Wycliffe's letters. More than ever before Lily's chair buzzed up and down the lanes. She got a new Union Jack pennant to replace the old one from her bicycle. It could be seen fluttering on every day of the week as she went on a round of farmhouses and cottages, to help in the knitting comforts for the fighting lads. People were constantly anxious to hear news of Wycliffe, who was going from success to success and, being a natural leader of men, was soon promoted to the rank of corporal. Tattoo Lily felt as though the two stripes were on her own arm as the farmers' wives and daughters helped her into their fire-bright kitchens. She missed her son, but the loss was salved by the frequency of his letters.

Lily lived for the advent of the postman. A thrill of delight, almost as if she had been kissed, never failed to run through Lily when she saw Wycliffe's grand writing on the envelope. In the mornings she would wait up the orchard path just to see the postie pushing his bicycle up the bray. At the slightest indication that he was going to stop by the house, she was down by the gate in a flash, leaving a faint blue cloud of exhaust to disperse under the apple trees. Such powerful letters did Wycliffe write that she had to open them there and then, and inform the postman of the principal items so that he could carry the titbits along the road to her Protestant neighbours.

Then one day came a letter which caused Lily a flutter of another sort. Wycliffe was courting, courting strong. Lily was not the slightest bit jealous, but nevertheless a ripple had run across the still pool of her relationship with Wycliffe. Of course her boy must obviously marry sooner or later. At times, before he joined the army, she had been rather frightened by the way he changed from girl to girl so that she never knew whom he would be bringing into the house next. No, Tattoo Lily was convinced that Wycliffe would get the pick of any crossroads, even in England. He was made for rolling in the bog—anyone could see that. Despite requests for more details about the girl, which Lily made in her replies, Wycliffe said almost nothing about her though he was obviously very much in love. The reason for his reticence was made clear by a further letter from London. So white did Tattoo Lily go, such quivering seized her lips, that the postman thought that Wycliffe had written to say he was wounded or even dying. But Lily passed it off and returned more quickly than usual to the house. That something was up without a doubt the postman knew for certain, and he said so to Lily's neighbours, for she had not given him the usual bits of news to pass on. But Lily never divulged the news of that letter. Wycliffe's girl was a Papist.

Nothing he wrote in subsequent mail could convince his mother that this was not a major national disaster. Try as he would by the might of the pen to explain that English Romanists were entirely different from the local Fenians at home, nothing could change his mother's attitude. The whole black-hearted lot of them, she wrote, served the Pope and he, God knows, was Britain's greatest enemy. None of Wycliffe's patient remonstration, all trying to convince his mother that neither the girl, her family, nor their Catholic friends had the slightest wish to shoot the King and replace him with one of their own kind, had any effect on Tattoo Lily. How could her son, she wrote, ever believe a word said by a Catholic, when he knew as well as she did that they could easily tell a lie and pay half-a-crown at the next confession and get it forgiven?

The shock of Wycliffe's intention to marry a Papist had a two-fold effect on Tattoo Lily, the event itself and the terrible blow her fame would suffer and the humiliation she would undergo if word of it ever leaked out. She, pride of the county, consort to members of parliament, the mother of a son married to a Papist! Such a thing was not to be contemplated. Not even the bicycle accident had made Lily so feel ill. Here was a canker gnawing her and nothing could be done. She could not even relieve her pain by telling somebody of its cause. Tattoo Lily had never been obliged to grapple with mental anguish before. It was an invisible worm eating the heart out of her beautiful rose, and in the end her body began to suffer in sympathy with her soul. On some days the pains in Lily's belly were so acute and the sickness so vile that she could not get out of bed. Her friends rallied and waited on her hand and foot giving her soothing medicines from the chemists, because Lily refused to see a doctor. She understood only too well that doctors were no good for the curing of *her* ills. More misery than ever lay in store for her, however. In spite of entreaties and pleadings and many a tear-soaked letter, Wycliffe remained adamant, and at length sent the fatal letter announcing his wedding day. But that was not half of it. Wycliffe was undergoing instruction and would be received into the Catholic Church. Lily took to her bed at once and nothing would induce her to come out of it. She was too bitterly ashamed to face her brethren at Lodge meetings, or even to follow the daily round and common task of her life.

Besides unhappiness, time now came to torment Tattoo Lily. She lay in bed watching autumn winds blow the curtains, winds which brought the dank smells of dying leaves, winds with a chill touch that hinted of winter. There were hours now to pass, waiting for the pain to wash over her like the waves of the cruel sea. Between the worst attacks, Lily's mind probed and searched into the years of Wycliffe's childhood. She brought every incident to the light of day again, resurrected every word, kind or angry, she had ever said to him, trying to find the crack which now had brought him down to ruin in his prime. And this intense analysis produced results, for Lily began to see certain things in a new light, and she was angry with herself for having failed to see the true meaning at the time.

In the early blissful years when Wycliffe had been such a comfort to her in her widowhood, Lily could find nothing ugly or sinister. And yet, a closer scrutiny showed that even then there had been something a little odd about the boy. From a baby he had shown a love of candles. And when he grew old enough to have a turnip lantern for Hallowe'en, he had always insisted on keeping it afterwards. He would light them in his room, and lie for hours in his bed, hypnotised by the mellow rays bursting out of the eyes and the mouth of the gutted turnip. It would be quite shrivelled before he would part with it for his Chinese lantern at Christmas, and all this in spite of Lily having got the best Tilley lamps from Belfast. Lying in her bed, desolate within and hopeless without, Tattoo Lily remembered Wycliffe's antics on wet days or when he was tired of toys or friends. He would go to the barn and climb into a large, disued meal-ark. He closed its great lid on top of himself and in perfect contentment sat in the meal-ark with the warm flickering light of candles for company. Lily had never approved of this, but since it afforded Wycliffe such pleasure, and she could think of no reason to forbid him, she allowed it to continue. But seen now in the light of his desertion to the evils of Rome, the boy's habit smelt of popery. Perhaps spies from Maynooth had even got hold of the child in those days and filled him with insidious notions, spies who would stop at nothing to gain their ends.

Not a chink of comfort could Tattoo Lily see in all the darkness engulfing her. As she plundered the treasure of Wycliffe's childhood she came upon more and more indications of later events. For a birthday gift Lily had once given him a box camera, but Wycliffe was not wild with delight as she had hoped at this very superior kind of present. He was undoubtedly pleased but did not immediately rush out and photograph everything within sight. He would wait, Wycliffe told her solemnly, until something specially interesting came along. And what had it been but to snap the byreman's daughter on the way home from her Popish confirmation. Following quick on her vision of the little girl passing the gate all dolled up in her white finery, the answer to the whole of Wycliffe's perversion suddenly flashed upon her. Tattoo Lily sat bolt upright in her bed now that she had discovered the root cause of all Papish intrigue. It had happened at old Maggie Maguire's funeral to be sure.

The funeral had also passed the gate and the topiary hedge, for on spotting the procession's approach, his mother had sent Wycliffe into the front to bang his Orange drum. Every detail of the scene stood clear before Lily now. To silence drum and drummer, the bold cub who was holding the priest's holy water had liberally sprinkled Wycliffe. Whether the hair on the holy water brush really had come from the white beard of Pontius Pilate as the Catholics claimed, Lily could not be sure. But she was sure that from this moment her son's soul had been tarnished, its Orange brightness lost, perhaps forever, by that unholy baptism. What good to him were the two stripes on his arm and his body of fine muscles, now that the red woman of Rome had captured his soul? When the postman brought the letter from Wycliffe in which he said that he had been received into the church, Lily plumbed new abysses of misery. She drank herself to sleep with whiskey half hoping that her eyes would never open in this wicked world again.

But just as the deepest, blackest part of the night is said to precede the dawn, so another letter came shortly afterwards marking a signal victory for the Orange cause. Wycliffe's girl had jilted him. She brought him to the brink of hell and then deserted him. Immediately she finished reading the letter, Lily got up, dressed and set off in her wheelchair for the town. She went straight to the post office and drew out a whole ten pounds from her savings account and posted it to Wycliffe so that he could wet his whistle in celebrating. The sickness of the last months dropped from Lily and she felt well enough to attend a Lodge meeting that very evening. Being so shy, Wycliffe had never held correspondence with anybody else in the neighbourhood so Lily felt quite assured that no one would know the history so far.

Within the space of a few months Wycliffe had been drafted

abroad and was taken prisoner by the Japanese. At first the full significance of this was lost on Lily. Her conception of cruelty had never gone beyond the outrages she attributed to the Fenians, and her conception of foreigners in the world's hot regions was that they all wore grass skirts and were heathen. Other than this she had no idea at all of what was involved, which was a merciful blessing because Wycliffe was labouring naked in the sun on a railway in Burma. His muscles had fallen away, his body was a skeleton shrivelled up like the Hallowe'en turnips. Only one thing in him remained unchanged, his eyes. Though often bright with fever, the blue clear, dreamy gaze of them never altered. But in spite of the eyes, Tattoo Lily would never have recognised Wycliffe, if by a miracle he had come up the cottage bray.

He dreamed all the time of such a miracle. His capacity for withdrawal, for regarding the real things about him as less than real, now saved him. As the rail track crept along, growing like a steel snake through the tropical forests, each of its sleepers seemed to be the gravestone of a soldier, for indeed those that died had no stones. Wycliffe's fellow prisoners marvelled at his equanimity, at the indestructible fibre of spirit within him. He took it for granted that he should do the work of two if another man was sick. He never questioned that his ration should go to another more hungry than he, and he kept his sores a secret as long as possible. Of course, when he could no longer stand up on his ulcerated feet and actually fell on the ground, he could hardly conceal it any more.

Other men cursed their captors and their cruelty and talked incessantly of what they would do if they ever got home again, if ... But Wycliffe rarely spoke and when he did it was never about the Japanese, nor about home and the future. He felt no need to utter aloud the things he thought of continuously. Dreams cannot be translated into words. While the ringing of the sledgehammer stole over him like hypnosis, Wycliffe would sail away, free and disembodied. He changed the menacing green of the jungle for the green hills of home. And when they struggled at night by the light of bamboo flares, he exchanged this cruel light for the soft light of remembered candles and flickering shadows in the meal-ark and in the byre when they milked on dark winter evenings. They were dry tears that Wycliffe shed when he wondered if the four-sisters would be lifting their hundreds of bright eyes on the lake islands to an enamel sky, lake islands where the bantam-grebe and mirokey broke the stillness with soft calls, and high, descending trills. But as the music of his youth broke over him, none was sweeter than the remembered drumming of God's goat, and the cracked, clinging clash of the Catholic Angelus bells carried hither and thither by the wind.

Dry tears and silent thoughts, those were the means by which Wycliffe chose to endure the years of sweat and disease, hunger and thirst in the tropics. Had he wished, he could have joined the other Ulstermen when they reassured themselves by the singing of Orange songs or the swapping of tales which told about many a bygone Twelfth of July. The fact that he had all but married a Papist girl and that he had himself joined her church had nothing to do with his reluctance to sing with the others. The Orange songs simply reminded him of his boyhood when his mother had sent him into the garden to bang his drum and frighten the Catholic drovers' animals. And he had always hated it so much, and the mad way his mother behaved over anything to do with Orange things, he could not bear to be reminded of it. From quite early years he had decided that as soon as he was old enough he would take the King's shilling and escape from it. Having done so, he had no intention of connecting himself with such things again. Wycliffe wanted nothing in the world so much as to be left alone, in quiet, and in peace. He already knew what he would do if he ever got home again, if ... Money, sprees, night-love in the hedges, the centuries-old Orange hates meant nothing to him any more. If asked to say what the Japanese prison camps had done to him, Wycliffe would have said they prepared him for life.

After Wycliffe was captured, letters from him stopped

abruptly and for a long time Tattoo Lily did not know whether
he was alive or dead. The old postie felt guilty that he passed the
gate so often with nothing in his bag for the woman who waited
there, without fail, every time he came up the bray. When at last
a trickle of news began to come through, Lily had already aged.
The proud flame of her hair died and was soon as grey as a
badger's. When the loneliness in her heart was unbearable, Lily
took to bed and bottle and would stay there for days on end. The
whiskey bloom on her nose grew from a suspicion to a
confirmation of suspicions. But she never doubted but that one
day her own Wycliffe would be home, a hero once more. So
when VJ Day came Tattoo Lily was not in the least surprised and
told every one that her son would soon be home. She went off
to a victory night supper and headed the table and received a
dozen toasts as mother of the local hero.

Tattoo Lily was not sure what Wycliffe's appearance would
look like when he did come home to the cottage again. Thin,
perhaps, she thought, and older. But she could form no exact
picture. Lily could not really recall his face as it looked on the
day he went away to Omagh. Only snaps from the box camera
served to remind her. It seemed to Lily as though interminable
months passed before Wycliffe was in Britain again although in
hospital. But at least letters could pass between them now
without fear of their going astray. His mother showered him with
letters, and because he was ill did not expect too many in return.
Each one, however, was treasured because they were like
promissory notes, for Wycliffe himself would soon come home
and tell her everything that had befallen him in the intervening
years. The letters from hospital were mere notes, but when his
strength returned Wycliffe wrote properly to Tattoo Lily and
told her of his intentions. Only his faith, he said, had carried
him through the dread years. With every worthless thing
stripped from him, only that had remained, rock-like in the
desert. On leaving hospital and crossing to Ireland again,
Wycliffe was going to enter a monastery.

Lily thought she was reading a death sentence. And then it

occurred to her that, of course, the boy's mind was turned, his poor brain was wandering, the war experiences had been too much for him. Lily wrote to the hospital voicing her opinion and demanding that they send him home at once to her for she would look after him until such time as his right mind returned. The hospital officials replied with a short note which stated that, as far as they knew, her son's mental condition was unimpaired, and that his discharge from the hospital and from the army would take place as soon as his physical health would permit. So Lily was left to contend with Wycliffe alone. She had thought that being jilted by the Romanist girl would have knocked some sense into her son's head. After all he had suffered how could he think of monasteries and the like where not only were orgies held (Tattoo Lily had only a faint idea of what an orgy was) but babies were buried in quicklime down in the cellars.

Wycliffe was as deaf to her threats and entreaties as he had been over the girl. He was going to a monastery and that was that. Lily now began to burn in Orange indignation. With such ideas in his head, it was all too clear that Wycliffe could not come home to a good stout-hearted Protestant welcome. In her mind's eye Tattoo Lily had already planned Wycliffe's homecoming, down to the last square inch of red, white and blue bunting. Not to have all that would be a great disappointment. Wear the King's uniform he might, but Wycliffe could never dare show himself in the county and let it be known that he was about to enter a monastery. Lily also burned with a mother's passion for her son. She longed to rush and warn him of all the scheming ways of the Papists of whom he had fallen foul. It was almost certain that Tattoo Lily would never see him again if he remained stuck like a limpet on the rock of that faith. Then Lily read in a newspaper that a young turncoat soldier in Belfast had been stripped, tarred and feathered and tied to a lamppost. Suppose this should happen to Wycliffe if he came home from England! She wrote quickly then that he was *not* to come home and told him why. As for the neighbours, she told them that Wycliffe was doing a strong line with a girl across the water.

Wycliffe wrote a final missive to his mother after all arrangements had been made. He told her of the enclosed monastery in the Free State where he would be able to live the quiet life of contemplation and prayer that his soul craved. Such expressions of mystical longings passed over Lily's head, she merely interpreted them as another way of saying that Wycliffe had been kidnapped. Nobody would go to such a place except under force, she thought. Without actually willing it to come, a plan began to take shape in Lily's mind. Not since the bold hussy had introduced Wycliffe to Popish smells and Peter pennying had she seen her boy. Lily counted the years and was surprised at their number. But in spite of them and all that had happened Lily was still convinced that one look from her good Protestant eyes and, if needs be, a quiet sob on her Wycliffe's broad shoulder, would break the Romanist chains that held him. This Tristan and Isolde kind of a look became first an idea, then an obsession with Lily. It grew from a mere wish to a plan of action. Though she were die in the attempt, Tattoo Lily determined to see her son again and prove her Orange worth.

Lily determined to visit her son and attempt some kind of *coup*. Not a whisper of her intentions leaked out for she confided them to no one. A few days before the departure she had a man in to oil the wheelchair and overhaul its engine. She loaded the chair with essential food and clothes for her journey and concealed a revolver under one of its cushions. And one morning, before even the postman came, Tattoo Lily was away up the second-class road, and not a soul in the whole townland knew she was gone.

She drove her chair at rather a dangerous speed to the nearest railway station. She knew she could get into the guard's van as she had often done so when travelling to Twelfth of July meetings. In no time at all she came to the Border and was over it like some ancient crusader. But the train moved at a snail's pace most of the way and it was not much before sundown that Lily, chair and all, were set down at their journey's end. Her final objective lay another five miles away and with undimmed hopes

Tattoo Lily went bumping along the green lanes of high summer. Lily was surprised to see how clean the countryside looked and how like their own country. Under the last of the day's sun it smiled benignly and try as she would Lily could find nothing sinister. She could not find even one child wearing the wooden shoes of Popish slavery.

Ballybogelly was a small village which existed solely because the monastery did, and like the Cheshire Cat's grin, it, that is the monastery, could well have existed without the cat, that is the village. Not that Ballybogelly was altogether a one-eyed affair. In addition to many cottages being occupied by familiars from the religious house it boasted other amenities of civilisation. It had, for instance, a hotel, though in this case 'hotel' was used as a collective noun to describe the building which housed the post office, the undertaker's, and the grocer's, besides the bar and guests' rooms. All this could be found under the one roof, or rather under a series of roofs, for, as may be imagined, the building had grown gradually, bits and pieces being added according to need.

Tattoo Lily found the hotel. Her arrival caused the entire secular population of Ballybogelly to turn out leaving their assiduous labours. At least ninety per cent of this population had never seen a wheelchair before, let alone one propelled by an internal combustion engine. That such a chair could be used as a major mode of transport left them speechless, not because it did not amaze them but because they had no previous experience on which to base comments. Yet in spite of the spectacular way in which she burst upon Ballybogelly, no suspicion was admixed with the curiosity she roused. Ballybogelly was truly cosmopolitan despite its pitiful size, for it never asked questions of any strangers about anything. Visitors to the monastery came frequently, and if not accommodated within its walls then they stayed at the hotel.

Needless to say, Tattoo Lily was no guest of the Reverend Guest master, so she decided that she would come to no harm in the hotel. Within minutes of wheeling through the door she

realised that they served excellent porter. That at least was a
comfort, and its relaxing influence sent her to bed for an early
night. Next morning Lily was up betimes. She took a hearty
breakfast for such a lot was destined to happen that day and she
could face none of it on an empty stomach. Certain plans could
not be settled until Tattoo Lily had surveyed the lie of the land.
Before leaving home she had realised it would be quite
impossible to go up and bang on the monastery front door and
demand to see her son. Having seen the monastery gatehouse
now, Lily knew this to be even more true. However, it would
take a good deal more than scheming Mickeys to keep Lily down
and had there been a dozen doors she would achieve her aim
somehow. Even if women were admitted, which Lily knew not
to be the case, they would never allow her and Wycliffe to be
alone. Secret eyes would be watching and secret ears listening.
Oh, yes, Tattoo Lily was wise to the ways of Romanist convents.

By some inherited military skill, the same fearlessness in
battle which had driven James the Fleeing from Irish shores, Lily
knew that trying to breach walls was useless compared with
simply getting the gates opened from the inside. But in her
particular case it would be quite unnecessary for her to go
personally within the walls. What she had to do could be done
without that. Wycliffe would be helped not at all if his mother
was to end her life abruptly in a lime pit in the cellar. With great
wiles and subtlety, Lily laid her plans. Fate played into her hands
in the shape of an informer, who did not even know what
valuable information he was giving to Lily. He came into the
hotel bar and sat noisily sipping porter through a web of
drooping moustache. He was, it appeared, in the monastery's
employ as a gardener. Descending like a wolf on the fold, Tattoo
Lily plied him with free drinks, getting in exchange from the all-
but-unconscious old man, the complete layout of the monastery.
Before they left the bar, Lily had a mental plan of the place, as
smartly drawn in her head as any architect could do on paper,
despite grand measuring rods and the like. For a few drinks more
the old man offered to push Lily round the place, and he did so,

pointing out not only its salient features but its intimate details as well. He thought that Lily must be specially interested in the holy well which stood outside the monastery wall.

Everyone who came to Ballybogelly was interested in the holy well, he said, pushing Lily near it. All her Protestant hackles rose at this impertinence and she was not a little fearful that the holy well might cast some sort of evil spell over her. Yet a greater purpose had to be fulfilled on that day, and she must endure all this for his sake, that is, Wycliffe's. She allowed the man to wheel her sun-wise round the well and to fill her bottle with its water. Lily even let her good Ulster linen handkerchief be tied to the fairy thorn, though she stoutly refused to make the sign of the cross on the stone by the well. That would have been like sticking a dagger straight into her heart. As she was a cripple in a chair the man saw the difficulty she would have and did it for her, so saving Lily from exposure as a Protestant infiltrator.

The morning was glorious and it seemed as though the sun would never stop climbing into the blue. Presently, Tattoo Lily dismissed the man with more money for drinks, when he had pointed out the exact spot by the wall where she wanted to be. Behind the wall were the tiny gardens of individual cells, and behind the position where Lily's chair now stood was Wycliffe's own garden plot and his own cell. In his final letter Wycliffe had told his mother that his name in religion would be Brother Emmanuel, and she, of course, realised that his own good Protestant name would not be tolerated within the conventual walls. So now Lily had been able to ask the old man which was Brother Emmanuel's place without rousing suspicion. As soon as the man disappeared inside the hotel, Tattoo Lily moved away from the holy well and stopped her engine as she approached the wall for fear of attracting attention from the wrong people. She wheeled herself into position, and made sure that nobody was watching her.

A passer-by might have thought from the way that Lily kept looking at the top of the wall that she was a naturalist studying the movements of a butterfly. Tattoo Lily was doing nothing of the sort, but was measuring the wall's height with an exact eye. She judged it not to be excessive for her purpose and was glad because it seemed one more sign that the God of all Orangemen was on her side. Whatever other physical faculties Lily may have lost during her life, her sense of aim was not one of them. This had remained as accurate and reliable as in the far-off days when she had emptied slops on the heads of Fenian interlopers. And her aim was now about to restore her lost son to her. Among the stores she had packed on the shelf under the wheelchair's seat was a packet, well-wrapped in brown paper. It contained a suit, so that Wycliffe could make an escape in respectable clothes. With nice balance and perfect poise, Lily threw the parcel. It sailed upwards in a neat parabola, curved over the top of the wall and landed with a scarcely audible thud on the farther side.

Lily waited a few moments. Not a sound disturbed the morning stillness. Making sure that she was still unobserved, Tattoo Lily took out a leg of chicken. She had not forgotten her boy's weakness fro a nice bit of fowl. From a pocket Lily pulled out a piece of string. To the chicken she tied a copy of Mr. J.A. Kensit's great book on 'a Protestant Pilgrimage to the Pope's headquarters'. Faced with the evidence of what Mr. Kensit found in Rome, Wycliffe would see revealed the wickedness he had fallen into. With a deft movement Tattoo Lily sent leg of chicken and book over. Tense and alert she waited for some response from the other side of the wall. But nothing disturbed the cloistral calm. As perhaps the most powerful form of bait, to be used if all else failed, Lily had brought Wycliffe's old pipe. This was the one with the top that he had been so fond of, as it kept the rain out while he was clipping the Orange topiary in the good old days before he sold himself to the devil.

Lily had ever been impatient of results of her work, and people always wondered from where, apart from sheer loyalty, she found enough patience to keep the famous hedge. Now that nothing happened after she had flung Wycliffe his pipe, she shifted restlessly in her chair. Perhaps Wycliffe was at some Popish business in the church for faint sounds of music reached her. Certainly it did not sound like a bawl of a staunch Protestant hymn, though she failed to recognise the powerful simplicity of plainsong. Tattoo Lily had never been known to give up any undertaking once begun. Now she resolved not to budge from the wall until developments took place.

Reflected warmth from the wall struck Lily comfortably. She lifted her face to a hot sun, and hidden larks trilled madly. Bees hummed in the air, heavily laden with their bog harvest, giving the final note of rhapsody and laziness to the day. At first Lily only nodded and she caught herself doing it. But the early pints of creamy porter in alliance with the sun proved too strong for her, and in no time at all she fell asleep.

Ballybogelly never really woke up on a normal day. Certain movements were observable early in the morning which could be translated as getting up and starting work, and a similar process in reverse, not too late at night, could be interpreted as going to bed. But on the whole, the village never really woke up and after the morning's first exertions, actually grew sleepier and sleepier as the day wore on. This pattern had been unchanged for centuries, and was also the reason why its inhabitants lived to an immoderate old age. Ballybogelly never felt really secure unless, at any one time, it had two living centenarians. At that particular time, Ballybogelly had only one and he was in the hotel having his morning porter, when the landlord burst into the bar. The barmaid was just pulling another pint for the monastery gardener. But at the sight of the landlord, she dropped the glass, porter and all. He was as white as a ghost. Such speed as that with which he dashed into the bar, such violence of emotion that he displayed had not been seen in Ballybogelly, the centenarian confidently affirmed, in a hundred years. When breath returned to the landlord and he could control speech, he bade them double up to the attic and look through the skylight where they would clap eyes on a sight the like of which none of them had ever seen nor was ever likely to see again, either in Ballybogelly or anywhere else on God's earth.

It was the greatest miracle in all Ireland, in all the world, he kept telling them as they charged up the stairs. And it had happened in poor little Ballybogelly.

None of them stopped to argue with the landlord, or cast doubts on his assertions, or ask for details of what had happened, as people usually did. Normally in Ballybogelly you had only to repeat in the hotel bar that you chanced to meet so-and-so and that together you talked about such-and-such, for everyone automatically to call you a liar and demand a complete reconstruction of the event, with adequate proof and witnesses before they would begin to believe that there might be a grain of truth in your claim. So for the landlord to come in, say that he had just witnessed a miracle, and for everybody to take him immediately at his word and put themselves out to go and see for themselves, shows what a state the landlord was in. And no wonder, for what they all saw from the skylight was the cripple from the wheelchair, running and dancing, and skipping about on the hill. Unmistakably it was Tattoo Lily, out of her chair, as free as a new-born lamb.

When sufficiently recovered to explain what had taken place, the landlord said that earlier he saw Lily drinking water from the well, a well that, after all, had been given its miraculous powers in AD 541 when St. Senanus passed that way and bathed his blistered feet in its water. If any miracles had happened in the fifteen centuries since, none could have been so spectacular as the sight of Tattoo Lily leaping out of her chair with a yell and tearing away up the hill with a cloud of white dust behind. The landlord had just been walking by the well back to the hotel when it happened.

Having seen the miracle through the skylight, the barmaid and the gardener, the landlord and the centenarian flung themselves downstairs and up towards the dancing figure on the hill, shouting and calling for the other Ballybogellyians to drop whatever they were doing and join them. A score or so of people dashed from their cottages and trailed the landlord who was now in the lead. Nobody paid any attention to the empty wheelchair by the monastery wall, nor to the centenarian who was sorely tried by the hill's steepness. One and all wanted to be the first in kissing Tattoo Lily's hands, for she was undoubtedly well on the way to becoming a saint. Certain of the religious familiars were disturbed by the shouts of the procession running by their cottage doors. They came out also, and while some dashed over to the monastery, the others joined the straggle of figures running up the hill. In a moment the monastery gate was thrust open and hooded monks streamed out, their white habits flapping like demented swans. The whole of Ballybogelly wanted to see the miracle woman.

And see her they did indeed. A completely new Lily stood on the hill brow contorting herself, doing a yogi-like series of exercises to prove mainly to herself but also to the witnesses, that her legs were in perfect condition. Tattoo Lily was not only renewed in body, but in soul too. In her excitement and joy she forgot all about both Protestant and Catholic causes, as she pirouetted and did knee-full-bends before astonished lay and clerical onlookers. Then suddenly she stood stock still, and such an expression stole over her that half the people thought the miracle was over and the other half thought she was in the process of having a vision of the Virgin. Several monks sank to their knees, as Lily's arms rose slowly in an extended position. A smile of beatification transformed her face as one of the monks stepped towards her. Even the strange garb and the shaved head could not disguise her Wycliffe. The crowd, now grown to more than a hundred strong, watched them weep in each other's arms. Round the well a similar crowd clustered and almost fought to get a cupful. The water was pretty low. Now that there was no longer any doubt that the key which had unlocked Lily's limbs had come from the healing properties of the blessed waters, many had been drinking copious draughts.

All this happened so quickly that it did not occur to Tattoo Lily that she ought to explain what, in fact, had actually taken place, and it certainly did not enter the heads of the observers to ask. So far as they were concerned the thing was a miracle, and therefore no questions need, or indeed ought, to be asked. Already, from Lily's own mind, the facts of the matter were beginning to fade. Certainly the dreams that haunted her as she slept in the chair had evaporated from her memory, except that they were something to do with a Popish gunman who chased her along endless corridors of a nightmare monastery. When he had fired, she saw the flash from his gun and felt the bullet strike her brow. Tattoo Lily had screamed and clapped a hand to her forehead. Something inside her was released and she fled from the dream-monastery into the sunshine outside. Her legs could now move fast enough to carry her beyond the gunman's reach. And as she ran, hand on forehead feeling the stickiness of blood, Tattoo Lily realised that she was really awake, really running, and that the stickiness on her forehead was not blood from a gunshot wound, but only a bird's dropping. Lily did not understand, of course, that the shock from the bird who came to sit on the wall just above her, had broken the nervous paralysis of all the past years.

Beset by so many people, excited by the recovery of two good legs and the reunion with Wycliffe, Tattoo Lily could not think clearly and the confusion was not helped by a few more glasses of porter. Before long she abandoned the effort to sort out the facts in her own mind and accepted Ballybogelly's general verdict that the holy well was responsible.

It was plain that something special had to be done with Tattoo Lily. She could not be left in the hotel like an ordinary visitor to Ballybogelly. So when the bishop was telephoned about the miracle he was asked if the sacred lady could be housed in the monastery. Of course, of course, said the bishop rather irritably because he had not thought of it himself. Without a beat of her Orange heart, without a twinge of Orange conscience, Tattoo Lily was conducted to a cool, comfortable room near the gatehouse. She cared for nothing now that she had her son and her health.

Before sunset the bishop was in Ballybogelly, conducting a *Te Deum* himself and leading a grand pilgrimage round the well.

Like fire through a wheatfield the news spread to Dublin and Maynooth, and when it was properly understood that none other than Tattoo Lily herself was involved, cars started out that very night, and soon not a spare place for parking could be found anywhere in the village. Before the monastery doors closed for that night more than a thousand people had been to pay a respectful court to Lily. Among the first was the barmaid from the hotel, bringing back the pound note and the shift she had stolen from the holy lady in the night.

For days Ballybogelly was in an uproar. At every opportunity the centenarian raised his voice in the hotel bar and said repeatedly that he had not seen the like in a hundred years. It became clear to Lily that Ballybogelly was her home now, and having a strong business head on her she decided that something must be done with her property north of the Border. It must be sold, cottage, topiary hedge, flowers and all. But since the miraculous doings in Ballybogelly could hardly have escaped the ever-sharp Orange ears of the North, it was necessary for Tattoo Lily to travel in secret to her house in order to set it ready for sale. Accordingly she was driven up through the night so that no Protestants should observe her arrival. Left alone in her thatched house once more, Lily danced through the rooms with delight. For over twenty years she had been quite unable to move freely or set a foot tapping on her kitchen floor where others had danced so happy and carefree at many a *ceili*. Faint echoes of bygone happiness rang from the now silent walls. She remembered Wycliffe running about the place as a tiny boy. What fruit now his strange habit of candle-burning had borne! An idea struck Lily and with her new-found agility she climbed on a chair and reached up to the dresser top.

Among the things stored there were Wycliffe's Chinese lanterns from past Christmases, a whole dozen of the flimsy coloured paper lamps. What a way to celebrate her life's climax, she thought, putting a candle in each lamp. Moving the chair, she hung them from bacon-hooks screwed generations ago into the kitchen ceiling beams, and lit the candles. How serene and bright they looked, these colourful lanterns swinging very gently and making the candle flames flutter like trapped moths. The cottage had never seemed more beautiful to Tattoo Lily. She opened yet another bottle of that grand whiskey they make in the Free State, and looked through the amber liquid at the lanterns. 'Beautiful,' she said aloud. Indeed that was Tattoo Lily's last thought and last word, because she was now as drunk as a fiddler's bitch and the happiest woman in all Ireland. And when the cottage was found in the morning, completely gutted by fire, nobody gave a thought to the Chinese lanterns, for not a trace of them remained.

Reaction to this disaster set in at once from both sides of the Border.

The Protestants stoutly declared that the Catholics had burned Lily in her bed, and for years now have been looking for IRA suspects to indict. And although everybody knew what took place in Ballybogelly, not one of her firm Orange friends ever believed that Tattoo Lily really became a turncoat. It was, they said, another example of vile Catholic propaganda from Dublin trying to get the Six Counties back. Other Orangemen produced the theory that Lily had died of a heart attack. They claimed that when the Mickeys came to retrieve her body they were so horrified by the tattooed Protestant slogans against the Pope that they decided to destroy it by fire.

Fortunately the conflagration left the topiary undamaged except for a singe here and there. As soon as everybody had recovered from the shock, a fund was started. The cottage ruins were organised into a tidy square of new lawn, and the rubble was made into a rock garden. And in the middle of this a fine bust of Tattoo Lily was erected, the whole memorial group being ceremoniously opened and unveiled by the finest quality in the land. So many people came to visit the place that a curator was appointed to a full-time job, which included keeping the garden trim with its showers of orange lilies and sweet williams, and clipping the topiary which, perhaps from the enrichment of the soil by the cottage's ashes, now began to sprout thicker and greener than ever before. Also included in the curator's duties was the sale, at sixpence a time, of postcards which showed Lily being decorated with her first tattoo.

Within a year the site became a place of pilgrimage for Orange brethren from the world over. To anyone who would listen, and this was nearly every visitor, the curator told the tale of what happened to Lily in heaven, and though this was not actually pronounced as an infallible dogma, it became nevertheless a generally accepted doctrine. As it says in the *Book of Revelation*, there are four-and-twenty seats reserved for the elders of the Protestants before the great white throne of God. And at the time of Lily's decease all these seats were occupied except one. And when Tattoo Lily came marching up the golden street of heaven it was King William himself who outran Sir Edward Carson to conduct the pride of Ulster to her place. At this point the curator would pause, and rightly so, for now that the two dozen seats were all filled, the end of the world could be expected at any moment. A not unimportant by-product of this piece of apocalyptic theology was the number of people who were getting themselves 'saved'.

As might be expected, quite a different interpretation of the basic event came from south of the Border, where the Catholics were utterly convinced that the Orange warmongers were responsible. After reading in the newspaper of her conversion and cure at the holy well they burnt Lily in her cottage, they said, as a reprisal. So soon as news of the fire reached Ballybogelly, plans were immediately put in operation by the authorities for Lily's beatification and, within a month, the proposals were lodged in Rome itself. Thousands of people began to pour into the village, so that with passing years its popularity rivalled old Matt Talbot's grave and then Lourdes itself. A convent was built by the holy well, placed symmetrically to match the monastery, and was given rights to deal in the special souvenirs. The barmaid, who stole Lily's pound and shift, sold her story to an American magazine, and took the veil. Within the convent's walls she was put in charge of the department producing plaster images of Lily in her wheelchair. Since, however, by some artistic ineptitude, the figures looked like Irish colleens and the wheelchairs like jaunting-cars, the souvenir shops in Belfast all unwittingly did a roaring tourist trade in them.

Following the fire, weightier matters had to be undertaken relating to the disposal of Lily's relics. Various learned ecclesiastical bodies from Dublin and further afield petitioned the Northern Government for the rights to these relics, for apart from the shift reverently framed in the monastery refectory and the wheelchair, little was left of the mortal Lily. At a lower level, there was considerable mirth in the South (particularly in the new, enlarged bar of Hotel Ballybogelly) about the Black North's version of what befell Lily in heaven, for every Christian soul knows that it is St. Peter who keeps the gate, and not Martin Luther. And on welcoming Lily, St. Peter certainly did not usher her into a chair beside the throne, because as he shrewdly observed, she has spent enough time sitting in her wheelchair.

The ultimate truth of these matters must wait to be revealed at the sounding of the last trump, but perhaps until then it is not altogether unsatisfying for Tattoo Lily to know that these contentions and the battle for her relics are likely to remain as big an issue as the Boyne Water itself.